CAUG

Fargo saw McGee's h... pistol. Fargo pumped two bullets into his face, one above the left eye and the second into his lower jaw, and dropped the man like a sack of brass doorknobs.

Fargo then turned to McGee's partner and said, "You'd be wise to crawl back into whatever rathole you call home, and right quick."

He then turned to the kid who had just taken a hell of a beating from the outlaws, and started to say, "I'd ask you if you're all right, but I don't hardly see the need—"

Fargo instinctively sensed the other outlaw make a move behind him. Fargo pivoted on his heel, swinging the Colt around, but knew it was too late. He saw the glint of the knifeblade, the burly man clutching it chest-high, half a beat from flinging it deep into Fargo's belly.

The Trailsman knew then that he was as good as dead. . . .

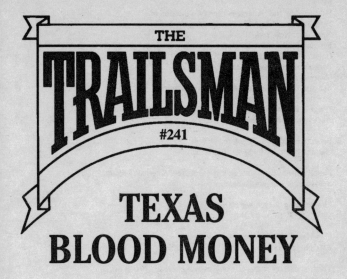

THE
TRAILSMAN
#241

TEXAS
BLOOD MONEY

by

Jon Sharpe

A SIGNET BOOK

SIGNET
Published by New American Library, a division of
Penguin Putnam Inc., 375 Hudson Street,
New York, New York 10014, U.S.A.
Penguin Books Ltd, 80 Strand,
London WC2R ORL, England
Penguin Books Australia Ltd, Ringwood,
Victoria, Australia
Penguin Books Canada Ltd, 10 Alcorn Avenue,
Toronto, Ontario, Canada M4V 3B2
Penguin Books (N.Z.) Ltd, 182–190 Wairau Road,
Auckland 10, New Zealand

Penguin Books Ltd, Registered Offices:
Harmondsworth, Middlesex, England

First published by Signet, an imprint of New American Library,
a division of Penguin Putnam Inc.

First Printing, November 2001
10 9 8 7 6 5 4 3 2 1

Copyright © Jon Sharpe, 2001
All rights reserved

The first chapter of this title originally appeared in *Frisco Filly,*
the two hundred fortieth volume in this series.

Ⓟ REGISTERED TRADEMARK—MARCA REGISTRADA

Printed in the United States of America

PUBLISHER'S NOTE
This is a work of fiction. Names, characters, places, and incidents either are the
product of the author's imagination or are used fictitiously, and any resemblance to
actual persons, living or dead, events, or locales is entirely coincidental.

The Trailsman

Beginnings . . . they bend the tree and they mark the man. Skye Fargo was born when he was eighteen. Terror was his midwife, vengeance his first cry. Killing spawned Skye Fargo, ruthless, cold-blooded murder. Out of the acrid smoke of gunpowder still hanging in the air, he rose, cried out a promise never forgotten.

The Trailsman they began to call him all across the West: searcher, scout, hunter, the man who could see where others only looked, his skills for hire but not his soul, the man who lived each day to the fullest, yet trailed each tomorrow. Skye Fargo, the Trailsman, the seeker who could take the wildness of a land and the wanting of a woman and make them his own.

Texas, 1859—
Where the pen is mightier than the sword
but the loaded gun is still the
mightiest of them all.

1

Skye Fargo was starting to get annoyed. Finally he turned to Eddie Buzzell, "You're crazy if you want to go any further. You might take a hunk of lead right between the eyes."

"I'm paid to take those kinds of chances, Mr. Fargo, just like you are," Buzzell said, and started scribbling in his damned notepad again. In the dark.

"Not these kinds of chances, Buzzell. Listen to me," Fargo said.

Eddie Buzzell listened. The man was a good listener.

"Those are the Danby boys camping down there in that dry wash," Fargo continued. "Three of the meanest, bushwhacking kill-crazy devils to draw breath in the state of Texas. Those boys've slaughtered, robbed, raped, and burned their way across the frontier. They—"

Damn it all, Buzzell was scribbling in his notebook again. That's all he ever did.

Buzzell said, writing furiously, " 'Robbed, raped, and burned their way across the frontier.' Beautiful. Then what?"

Fargo angrily snatched the notepad from Buzzell's hands and flung it into the bushes. Buzzell opened his mouth to protest, and Fargo clamped his hand over it, grabbing Buzzell in a very uncomfortable headlock.

"Listen to me, you ignorant New York pimplehead," he whispered into Buzzell's left ear. "The Danbys would just as soon blast your head off than spit on a bug. They're mean, Eddie, very mean. Ain't nobody been able to take 'em, not the Rangers, not the cavalry, not any of the twelve bounty boys they planted six foot under. But that's okay, Eddie, because I'm gonna take 'em myself. There's two thousand dollars apiece on their heads, dead or alive. That's six thousand dollars, my friend, just enough for a long and relaxing vacation anywhere I want. You ain't even carrying a piece, not that you'd know how to use it if you were. Be a good boy and stay right here till the shooting stops. I don't come back a minute later, I ain't at all. You hightail it back to town and get your skinny ass on a train back East. Them's the rules."

He released Buzzell, who went scrambling through the bushes to find his notepad.

"Make a little more noise, why don't you?" Fargo said.

Buzzell found his notepad and started writing in it again. "I won't get in your way, Mr. Fargo," he said. "You won't even know I'm here."

Fargo was satisfied that his firepower was ready. "It's your ass, Eddie, and I ain't responsible for it. You follow me in, you do it at your own risk. Whatever happens, just remember I tried talkin' you out of it."

"I appreciate that, Mr. Fargo," Buzzell said. "I really do. But I have my job to do, and you have yours. I can take care of myself."

"All right," Fargo said. "It's your funeral. Just—"

Shots rang out from what sounded like several directions, one of them whizzing so close that Fargo could smell the gunsmoke.

"Stay down," Fargo shouted at Buzzell, diving for cover in the bushes. Damn wet-behind-the-ears city punk had blown Fargo's cover. Fargo pumped the Henry twice in the direction of the belching gunfire down in the wash, and heard an audible grunt.

He slid like a greased snake through the thick underbrush in the direction of the silenced gunshots, clutching the shotgun in one fist. He circled the Danbys' campfire from eighty yards off, the fire deserted now, bedrolls empty. Shots were ringing out from behind him and off to the west now. The Danbys were firing blind, not hard to do on a dark night with no moonlight. Fargo had waited for a night just like this, knowing the Danbys weren't going anywhere. Issac had been spotted in a town called Swayzee three days ago, no doubt checking out the spoils.

A month ago, Eddie Buzzell showed up in town and began following Fargo around, asking questions and writing stuff down in that stupid little notepad. A journalist from New York City he was, and wanted to write about Fargo's many adventures for the magazines back East.

When Fargo got wind that the dreaded Danbys were sleazing around in his backyard and had a sizable bounty on them, he volunteered his services. Six thousand dollars was six thousand dollars, not to mention ridding the territory of the scurviest bunch of murderers since the Clantons.

And now here he was, pinned down by their gunfire. This wasn't going well at all, and he had Eddie Buzzell to blame.

He made his way over to a clump of live oak, leaned up against it, and began to reload the Henry. He knew he had to go to Plan B—trouble was, he had no Plan B.

He crawled silently toward a patch where the undergrowth was the thickest. Halfway there, he came upon the lifeless body of Willis Danby, a huge chunk of his neck missing, the last of his blood spurting into the dirt. His mouth was open, and Lord did he have a lot of rotten teeth.

It was one lucky shot, all things considered.

"Willis!" he heard one of the other Danbys bellow. He looked up and saw Issac Danby, all six and a half feet of him, charging down the wash, wielding a huge hatchet— taking Fargo's head off was his only goal in life.

"You killed him, you son of a whore!" Issac bellowed, and was on Fargo like beans on rice. He dived at Fargo, swinging the hatchet. Fargo ducked and rolled to the left, and Issac Danby landed on dirt.

There was no time to use the Henry, so Fargo let it fall from his fist. He jerked the six-gun out of his holster, but not soon enough. Issac pounced on him and curled his fingers around Fargo's gullet, squeezing with everything he had, filthy long fingernails digging into the soft flesh.

Fargo ripped at Issac's greasy black hair and came away with a chunk. Issac could have cared less. He kept squeezing Fargo's neck, successfully cutting off his air.

Fargo rammed his thumb into Issac's left eye, digging in deep until he felt flesh rupture. Issac wailed in agony, taking his hands from Fargo's neck and covering his face.

Fargo thrust up with his fist and slammed Issac Danby in the throat. Issac tumbled away, a gurgle, the likes of which Fargo would never forget, escaping him as he fell. It sounded as if somebody had slapped a slab of beef liver against a flat rock.

Fargo drew his pistol, trying to clear his head, and Issac pounced on him anew. Fargo managed to squeeze off one shot, which stopped Issac in midstep, taking him squarely in the gut. Issac dropped like a block of ice, but not for long. Even a solid gut-shot from five feet away couldn't keep a Danby down.

Issac rose to his knees and went for his Colt. A dark patch of blood covered half his face.

Fargo wasted no time in putting a second bullet into Issac Danby, this time right through his good eye, completely robbing him of his sight, along with half his face.

Blinded and beaten, Issac stood motionless. The Colt slipped from his fingers, but he did manage to stay alive long enough to pull out a shiny new pigsticker tucked into his belt with his other hand. He raised the knife a foot or so, then pitched forward into the dirt, raising a puff of brown dust, as dead as dead could be. The knife skittered across the ground a couple of feet from Fargo's foot.

"I'm getting too old for this," Fargo muttered. He sat up, rubbing his sore neck, and replaced the two bullets he'd put into Issac Danby.

He gave the barrel a spin, ready for action.

A shot barked behind him. Fargo saw the white blast of a pistol out of the corner of his eye. Pain exploded in his right shoulder. He went sprawling face first onto the ground. The Colt flew from his hand.

"Shit," Fargo growled, already in agony. A pair of dusty boots appeared before him. "I gotta say, I am very impressed."

There was no anger in the words, no malice. Fargo made himself look up, and found himself staring into the face of Earl Danby, one of the youngest of the Danby tribe. Just my luck, Fargo thought, feeling his life's juices squirting from his wounded shoulder.

"Who are you?" Earl Danby asked, tucking the twin barrels of his shotgun under Fargo's chin and raising his head up another few inches.

Fargo looked up at the younger Danby. He was smaller than his brothers, ferret-faced and scrawny, though Fargo had no doubts he was just as mean.

"I wanna look the man who killed my brothers right in the eyes," Earl Danby said, cocking his pistol and aiming it straight at Fargo's head. "Just so's the last thing he sees before he burns in hell is one of the Danby boys."

He aimed the twin barrels of his rifle in the middle of Fargo's forehead. Fargo squeezed his eyes shut. He'd failed, as he'd never failed before, and this particular failure meant certain death.

What a stupid way to die, Fargo thought just as he heard the dry click of Earl Danby's shotgun. Fargo's eyes opened wide. He still had a chance.

"Shit," Earl Danby said. He tossed his shotgun aside and went for his pistol. Fargo took the opportunity to roll to the left and go for Issac's knife.

Earl fired off a shot that kicked up dust an inch from Fargo's nose. Fargo snatched the knife, rolled onto his back, and flung it skillfully. He took the outlaw squarely in the balls.

Earl Danby let out a wail laced with pain, and yanked out the knife. Blood spurted from between his legs. He dropped his pistol and grabbed his wounded sweetmeats.

"Damn but that must hurt," Fargo commented, scrambling for Earl's gun. Earl sank to his knees, wailing like a stuck pig, and started whimpering like a little baby, trying unsuccessfully to staunch the flow of blood from his crotch.

Fargo didn't waste a second, snatching up the gun and scrambling to his feet. He aimed it directly at Earl Danby's head. Earl hardly seemed to notice, or even care, concentrating not on impending death, but rather the incredible pain from between his legs.

Earl Danby ceased to be, for the time being, an immediate threat to Fargo's health. Fat tears were rolling down his dirty face now, leaving clean streaks that Fargo could see even in the moonlight.

"Stop crying, Earl," Fargo said with a little heat. "It ain't becomin' to an outlaw of your stature."

"You shot my pecker all to hell, you stinkin' bastard," Earl Danby wailed, blood seeping through his fingers.

Fargo kept the gun trained on Danby's head. He wouldn't kill the last Danby brother unless he got stupid, which was a distinct possibility.

"I didn't shoot it, Earl," Fargo said. "Doubt I could find it if I tried."

"How'm I a-gonna get any women now?" Earl cried, clutching himself.

It was exactly the kind of question Fargo had expected from the likes of a Danby. He said, "Earl, havin' sex is about to become the very least of your problems."

He kicked Earl square on the chin, the tip of his boot connecting solidly with Earl's lower jaw. Still on his knees,

Earl flopped face first into the dirt, sickeningly dazed, but still conscious. Fargo hog-tied the bastard, rendering him harmless.

Earl spit out some dirt and said, "Stranger, the day's a-gonna come when I get me the chance to do to you what you done to me. Only thing is, I'm a-gonna cut your pecker off an' feed it to a dawg."

Fargo kicked Earl Danby hard in the ribs. Earl cried out in agony. Fargo grabbed him by the hair and yanked him forward, Earl screaming every inch of the way.

Fargo jabbed the barrel of the pistol into Earl's left ear. Earl whimpered.

"You make me feel tired all over, Earl," Fargo said. "I don't want any more of it. Behave yourself and maybe you'll live long enough to hang."

Fargo whacked Earl Danby on the side of his head with the business end of the pistol and left him facedown in the dirt.

"I had a friend with me, Earl," Fargo said, ready to adorn west Texas with the contents of Earl Danby's skull. "A fella from back East, name of Buzzell. You seen him?"

Earl Danby barely managed to shake his head, he was too busy blubbering like a baby. Fargo was just about disgusted. Time was when an outlaw worth his salt would accept his fate and still act like a man. Earl Danby was a disgrace to the memory of a lot of fast but dead hard cases that littered every Boot Hill in the West.

Fargo went looking and moments later found Eddie Buzzell flat on his back, deader than dead could be. A slug had taken out a nice chunk of his neck, and he'd bled to death in minutes. His eyes were open in an expression of disbelief. The notebook was still clenched in his left fist.

Fargo plucked the notebook from Buzzell and found the pencil in the dirt a foot or so away. Fargo started scribbling in the notebook, then tucked it into his vest pocket.

"I'm sorry, city boy. I tried to warn you. But you still

died in the saddle," Fargo said. He looked at the lifeless body with some affection and added, "You were a credit to your profession, Eddie."

Fargo went back to where Earl Danby was drooling into the dirt and pulled the Arkansas toothpick from his boot. He let Earl follow the razor-sharp blade with fearful eyes, teasing him enough with each movement to squeeze out some extra tears. Fargo pulled his arm back and in one fluid motion, swung forward. The trusted knife slashed the air and cut through the rope binding Danby's feet.

Fargo pulled tight on the rope shackling Earl's hands. "Get up, Earl," he said. "It's late and I'm tired."

Earl Danby grudgingly got to his feet. Fargo kicked him in the general direction of Mineral Springs. Earl started walking, and Fargo followed.

"You really think I'm a-gonna hang?" Earl wanted to know.

Feeling truly tired, Fargo said, "If the good people of Mineral Springs have anything to say about it, most likely."

Fargo gave Earl Danby another series of swift kicks the butt until Earl started moving a little faster.

2

"How long have you been with Livermore and Beedle Publications, boyo?" Phineas Huffington asked.

Huffington was a ruddy-faced, gin-swilling Irishman of fifty who was running—some would say galloping—to fat. Too many late nights at Delmonico's chomping the choicest steaks and gurgling the finest wines New York City had to offer. Phineas Hardy Huffington was also known for his ferocious temper, and had been known to toss many an employee of Livermore and Beedle out of his office window, which thankfully was only on the second floor of the Bowery building.

Dexter Tritt swallowed dryly. He said, "Two years, two months, three weeks, and four days, sir."

Huffington nodded, striking a match on the bottom of his shoe and relighting the cold cigar clenched in his teeth. He said, "What exactly is it you do for us, Tritt?"

"Well, I . . . I . . ." Dexter stammered. He'd never been called into Huffington's office before. Huffington was second only to Henry Livermore and Pendrake Roach Beedle themselves.

"Speak up, dammit," Huffington snapped. "I asked you a question, boy."

"Proofreader," Dexter said, his voice almost a whisper. "I proofread . . . that is, I check the galleys for mistakes . . ."

"I know what a proofreader does," Huffington said. "How much are we paying you, Tritt?"

"Six dollars a week," Dexter said. He was starting to perspire. Being nervous did that to him.

"How would you like to be promoted to staff writer?" Huffington asked. "Raise you up to eight dollars a week."

Dexter's eyes widened. "Staff writer?"

"What, you got wax in your ears?" Huffington said. "Eddie Buzzell was writing *Skye Fargo, Texas Town Tamer,* but he quit on us suddenly."

"Why?" Dexter asked.

"Who the hell knows?" Huffington snapped. "These things happen. Buzzell liked Texas so much, he decided to stay there forever. Point is, Tritt, we need somebody to take his place. You interested?"

Was he interested? Every night, Dexter stayed up until three or four in the morning—to the consternation of his widowed mother—tapping out Western yarns on a battered old typewriting machine he'd bought in a junk store for two dollars. Stories he hoped to someday get into print—into one of the forty or so distinguished publications tossed out monthly by Livermore and Beedle and their fifty-three employees.

There were *Romantic Western Yarns; Black Benny Penny, Border Ruffian; True Tales of the Untamed Frontier; Big Tim Savage, Comanche Killer* and about a dozen others with a total circulation of over 200,000 and growing.

That none of Livermore and Beedle's ten full-time scribes had ever been any further West than Tenth Avenue mattered not at all. From Portland, Maine to the Barbary Coast, men, women, and children alike waited anxiously for the next installment of *Burton Kennedy, Wyoming Trail Boss,* or *Ace Deuce Proxmire, Natchez Gambler.* Americans had an unquenchable thirst for any story set west of the Mississippi River.

Dexter knew *Skye Fargo, Texas Town Tamer* as well as anyone, had in fact read each of its thus-far six installments. That Skye Fargo—

"I see and hear everything that goes on around here, Tritt," Huffington said, and opened a drawer in his desk. Dexter half expected him to pull out a pistol, but instead Huffington now held a sheaf of papers in his fist. He tossed them on the desk.

"Go ahead," Huffington said. "Pick 'em up."

Dexter did, feeling dread like a hunk of ice in his belly. It was one of the stories he'd written late one night after everyone else had departed, one entitled *I Fought Off One Hundred Killer Apache.*

"You ought to be more careful where you leave stuff," Huffington said.

Dexter folded and refolded the pages, as if to make them disappear completely. Before he could, though, Huffington reached across his desk and snatched them back.

"Why so hasty, young Tritt?" Huffington asked. "I would say your literary efforts show great promise."

"They do?" Dexter said.

He was a tall, gangly lad of twenty, with a nose a little too large for his face, and a forehead that was already showing the first signs of a receding hairline. He was thin—too thin, his mother liked to moan—and tended toward nervousness. His Adam's apple bobbed furiously when he swallowed, and suits seemed to hang on him like wet drawers on a clothesline.

"So what do you say, Tritt?" Huffington wanted to know. "You interested or not?"

Dexter nodded vigorously. "Yes, sir, I'd like that a lot."

"Fine, good, then it's settled," Huffington said. He reached into his desk again, and this time he pulled out a bottle that contained a clear liquid that could have been water, though Dexter doubted it. The men at Donnegan's Saloon on Pacific Street drank stuff that looked just like it. They called it gin. Dexter had been there many a time, searching for his errant father. Huffington produced two very small glasses from the drawer and filled them with the spirited substance.

"What say we drink on it?" Huffington asked jovially.

Dexter had never taken a drink in his life, save for the sip of blackberry brandy his mother had given him once for a bellyache. He knew it was rude to refuse the man's offer, especially since the man was the vice president of the company that paid the rent on the cramped apartment Dexter, his mother, and his younger brother called home.

Huffington handed a glass to Dexter, and raised his own.

"To your health, Tritt," Huffington said, clinking Dexter's glass, and downed his in one gulp. Dexter took a small sip and felt the clear, burning liquid slide down his throat and come immediately back up. Try as he might, stifling the inevitable cough was near to impossible. Dexter sputtered, his face turning the color of pickled beets, and warm gin sprayed out of both nostrils. Before he could even recover, Huffington opened a humidor on his desk. Inside were a dozen or so big, black, smelly cigars nearly a foot long.

"Have a cigar, Tritt?" he asked. "The best money can buy, imported from Panama."

If the gin didn't kill him, the cigar most certainly would. Still, Dexter Tritt wanted more than anything to be a Livermore and Beedle staff writer, even if that meant smoking the stinky slab of foul tobacco. Dexter gently plucked a cigar from the humidor. Huffington struck a match for him, saying, "You're supposed to bite off the end."

Dexter, a stranger to cigars as well as gin, did just that. Not wanting to be so rude as to spit it on the floor or even have Mr. Huffington see him take it out of his mouth, Dexter chose to swallow it. Huffington lit the cigar. Dexter puffed furiously.

He smoked the cigar and the color of his face went from bright red to a pale shade of muenster cheese-green. He took another sip of gin. This one went down a little easier, but the effect, moments later, was extreme dizziness and a subtle hint of nausea. He started perspiring.

Huffington said, "You a married man, Tritt?"

"No, sir," Dexter said, trying to keep the room from spinning around.

"Got a sweetheart?" Huffington asked.

Dexter blushed, the green tint already present on his face now complimented by bright red. He finally looked up and said, "Not really. No, sir."

Of course, there was Rosie McNutt, the daughter of Roger McNutt, who owned McNutt's Cafeteria on DeKalb Avenue. Rosie was a raven-haired Irish beauty Dexter pined for from afar. She went with Norman Rosemont, the son of a Red Hook factory owner. Rumor also had it that they were engaged to be married. Dexter had never actually said a word her.

No, Dexter didn't have a sweetheart. Working days, supporting his widowed mother and twelve-year-old brother, and creating magazine yarns all night more or less squashed any hopes for a love life.

"Live in Brooklyn, don't you?" Huffington asked now.

"Yes, sir," Dexter said. "Herkimer Street, number 342."

"Brooklyn," Huffington said, looking somewhat nostalgic. "City of homes and churches. Broke a lot of heads in Brooklyn, I did, back when we were fighting the circulation wars for the Pennington newspaper syndicate. Got fifty cents a head for bashing skulls with a wood club, theirs and ours, it didn't matter. Half a buck was half a buck."

"Yes, sir," Dexter said. It was already past six. He'd told his mother he'd stop by Weinmeyer's butcher store to pick up the veal chops for dinner. His mother had taken to her bed with the flu that was sweeping through Brooklyn, so it was up to Dexter to maintain the household. That meant keeping his younger brother Harvey off the streets and out of trouble, a full-time job in itself.

"You're familiar with *Skye Fargo, Texas Town Tamer,* aren't you, Tritt?" Huffington asked.

"Yes, sir," Dexter said. "I proofread the first six install-ments."

"This magazine series has proven very profitable for Livermore and Beedle," Huffington said. "Our print runs have tripled between the first and last episodes, and the cir-culation is growing by leaps and bounds. We shipped 150 thousand copies of Fargo's last adventure a week ago. Big numbers. A lot of money, you betcha."

"Fargo and the West Texas Plunder, yes, sir," Dexter volunteered. "A fine piece of journalism."

"Whatever," Huffington said. "This Skye Fargo, he's one tough . . . one tough . . . what the hell they call a tough guy in Mexican?"

"A tough *hombre,*" Dexter said. "They call him an *hom-bre.* That's Spanish for—"

"Yeah, yeah," Huffington said. "Fargo's a tough little bastard. He's been giving us a hard time."

"You mean there really *is* a Skye Fargo?" Dexter asked. "We didn't make him up?"

"Shit no!" Huffington said. "And a bigger pain in the ass you ain't never seen. What have you heard about him, Tritt?"

"Just what I've read, Mr. Huffington," Dexter said. "He's been a lawman, a drover, lead a cattle drive up through Oklahoma Territory, killed a man in Fort Worth— that was from *Skye Fargo, Scourge of Hell's Half Acre.* Issue number three."

"Sounds right," Huffington said, and poured Dexter an-other large dollop from the gin bottle. Then he poured one for himself. Again he downed it in one shot.

"Drink up, pal," Huffington said. "The night is young."

Dexter chugged the contents of the glass. He started to feel a little giddy, light-headed. He took another puff from the cigar, and started to like it. All of a sudden, the world seemed like a nicer place.

"Like I was saying," Huffington said, pouring himself another. "This Skye Fargo has been giving us a hard time."

"Yes, sir," Dexter said, feeling pretty good.

"Skye Fargo was brought to our attention about two years ago," Huffington said. "By a friend of mine, Harry Hopewell. Hopewell's with the Pinkertons, out of Denver. Told me some wild yarns about a man named Skye Fargo. A real hard case, killed a fair number of men, and strikes fear into the hearts of those who cross him. Hails from Tennessee, or one of those places in the South. Went West and has probably stuck his fingers into every money pie there is. Slaughtered Indians, fought for Maximillian, taken on cattle barons, and God only knows what else. A true Western hero, Tritt, the kind even the brightest of Livermore and Beedle's bright writer boys couldn't dream up.

"He was ours, Tritt, and no mistake. Paid him a fair piece of coin to sell us his stories, and we've all been making money. Skye Fargo and yours truly. You understand what I'm saying?"

Huffington poured Dexter another. Dexter, not wanting to be rude, dutifully drank it.

"Yes, sir, I do," Dexter said.

"Good," Huffington said.

Dexter puffed a couple times on the cigar. It tasted a little better now.

"We recently received a wire from Texas," Huffington said. "A town called Paradise, to be exact. It was from Skye Fargo. Said a banker's check from the Paradise Savings and Loan was on its way back to us, every cent we paid him in the last year. Yesterday the check showed up, accompanied by a letter. You know what that letter said, Tritt?"

Dexter shook his head. Huffington's office began to spin even faster.

"He told us to go burn in hell, that's what it said,"

Huffington said angrily. "Skye Fargo said he didn't want to sell his adventures for money, said it made his life sound cheap. Can you believe that, Tritt?"

Dexter couldn't. He knew Livermore and Beedle paid Skye Fargo a very large sum of money. He'd heard others in the office talking about it.

"Said he wants nothing else to do with us, Skye Fargo did," Huffington said, and had himself another drink.

"That wasn't very smart, now was it?" Dexter agreed. He wanted more of Huffington's gin, but was afraid to ask. Huffington poured him another, as if reading Dexter's mind.

Dexter drank. He liked it, enjoyed the warm feeling of the gin rushing down his throat. All was well with the world.

"Last we heard," Huffington said, "Skye Fargo was doing whatever it is a man does out in Texas. He plays down his reputation as a gunslinger and ass-kicker, that we do know. And he wants nothing more to do with us, Tritt, told us to go away and leave him alone.

"Trouble is," Huffington said, taking another drink. "He's a moneymaker, Skye Fargo is, and Livermore and Beedle don't much like the prospect of losing him."

Huffington saw that Dexter's glass was empty. He filled it again and gave it to him. Dexter Tritt was feeling no pain.

"Ever been to Texas, boy?" Huffington asked, already knowing the answer.

"No, sir," Dexter said earnestly. Huffington would know if he was lying.

"Next Monday, young Mister Tritt," Huffington said, looking at a calendar on the wall, "you're going to Paradise, Texas, to talk to Skye Fargo. Try and make him see the errors of his ways, convince him that his future lies with Livermore and Beedle Publications. You understand me, son?"

Dexter gave it some thought. Mr. Huffington wanted

him to go to Texas, a distant land that existed only between the pages of Livermore and Beedle's ten-cent magazines. It was too much to even try and consider, especially not in his semi-inebriated condition.

Except that Huffington didn't give him a chance. He said, "You want to go to Texas or not? Almost double your salary? Because if you don't, we got half a dozen guys in your department who'd kill for the opportunity."

Dexter blurted out, "I'd love to go to Texas, Mr. Huffington, sir."

"That's just what I wanted to hear, Tritt," he said, picking up the gin bottle again and pouring the last of it into Dexter's empty glass.

"It's just that—" Dexter began.

"Just what?" Huffington asked, not smiling anymore.

"Well," Dexter said, "my father died five years ago, and I—I'm supporting my mother and my brother, you see, and—"

"Not a problem, Tritt," Huffington said. "We'll see to it that she gets your paycheck each and every week while you're gone."

"Well, that's fine, sir," Dexter stammered. "But there's also my—"

"Sweet limping Jesus!" Huffington thundered. "Do you want to be a staff writer or not, boyo?"

"Y-yes," Dexter said.

"Then we'll hear no more about it," Huffington said testily. "Stop down at the accounting office tomorrow. There's an envelope with the train tickets and two hundred dollars of expense money waiting for you."

Huffington rose. Dexter vaguely realized he was being dismissed. He rose from his chair, walked around from his desk, and pushed the office door open. He put his meaty hand on Dexter's shoulder and gave it a squeeze. Dexter winced. It hurt.

"Get Skye Fargo back for us," Huffington said. "We're

trusting you to get him to sign the contractual papers we've included in the envelope, Tritt. Get Fargo's signature, boy, and as God is my judge I'll see to it that you earn at least eight dollars a week for as long as you live."

Huffington added, "Fail to get Skye Fargo's signature on those contracts, Tritt, and Misters Livermore and Beedle will be very disappointed." He looked at Dexter sharply. "Very disappointed."

Huffington slammed the door shut. Dexter stood alone—and rather drunk—in the hallway. He was going to that magical land called Texas. In less than a week. Come to think of it, he'd never even been to New Jersey, much less Texas.

He turned to leave, when Huffington's office door opened and the big man stepped out. Had he had a change of heart? Dexter secretly hoped he had.

"Oh, and Tritt?" Huffington called to him.

"Yes, sir?"

Huffington said, "Don't forget to bring back receipts for everything. Misters Livermore and Beedle are very strict about expenses."

3

"So," Henrietta Tritt asked her oldest son, "is this Texas above or below Fourteenth Street?"

The veal chops were sizzling in their own fat. Dexter sat in the cramped kitchen while his mother pounded mashed potatoes in a huge pot, adding a lump of butter and some heavy cream every now and then. A smaller pot of green beans simmered on the stove. A loaf of freshly baked bread was already on the dining room table. Dexter's younger brother, Harvey, was nowhere to be seen.

Outside on Herkimer Street, children played kick the can, and women sat on stoops and peeled onions and potatoes for the evening meal and gossiped. The working men from the docks nearby were still trickling down the muddy, congested streets. The cry of Otis the fishmonger could plainly be heard above the rattle of the Atlantic Avenue trolley. Just another twilight in Brooklyn, New York, on a mercifully cool late-June evening.

"Texas is, well, to the west of New York, Mama," Dexter said, playing with a small carrot. His mother's concept of distances pretty much began and ended north of Delancey Street on Manhattan Island, south to Flatbush, and west to where the docks in Red Hook separated Brooklyn from New Jersey via the Harlem River. Due east was just more Brooklyn.

"Will you be back from this Texas in time for dinner, or should I just have some baloney ready if you get home late?"

Dexter sighed. His head was ready to split open after Huffington's cheap gin and smelly cigars, and his belly threatened to turn over whenever the aroma of frying veal chops wafted in his direction.

"Mama," Dexter said, "Texas is, well, it's pretty far away. I have to take a train. In fact, I have to take about six trains."

"Six trains?" Henrietta Tritt asked, turning from the stove and wiping her hands on a grease-stained apron. "Dexter, sweetheart, where is this Texas?"

Henrietta Tritt was a short, squat woman with curly white hair and a plump, pleasant face. The sin and downright evil that festered in the New York streets in which she had spent her entire forty-one years had failed to corrupt her, as she seemed more ignorant of life's harsh realities with each passing day.

Dexter had taken the liberty of purchasing a map of the United States of America on his way home at Brentano's bookshop. He folded it out on the kitchen table, and pointing with a pencil, said to his mother, "Here's where we are, Mama, in Brooklyn."

Henrietta Tritt stared down at the map, the first one she'd ever seen.

"That's Brooklyn?" she asked, wiping her hands on her apron. "It doesn't look anything like where we live."

Dexter let that one pass. He drew a line from New York west to Chicago. He said, "I take one train to Chicago, here, then another one to Kansas City"—he drew another line—"then another train down through Oklahoma Territory, and then all the way down here to Paradise, Texas, where Skye Fargo lives."

Henrietta said nothing and went back to mashing potatoes. "Dexter, you wouldn't be apt to be telling me a tale now, would you?"

"I leave in two days, Mama," Dexter said. "I've arranged

for the bookkeeper at the office to mail you my checks while I'm gone, so you don't have to worry about money."

Henrietta motioned impatiently for Dexter to clear away the map so she could set the table. She said, "I'm not too sure I like the idea of you going away all by yourself to this Texas place. Remember, Dexter dear, that you've never been away from home a single night by yourself, except for the time you took the trolley to visit your Aunt Inga and Uncle Ferd in New Rochelle last year."

This was true, Dexter thought. Secretly, he was growing more and more excited by the minute at the prospect of the epic journey he was about to make. Was it really anything like the stories he proofread every day, all gunslingers and savage Indians and shoot-outs in the middle of the street? And would the mashed potatoes in Texas be as good as his mother's?

"I really don't have much choice, Mama," Dexter said. "I have to see a man called Mr. Fargo and change his mind about some things. It really is a wonderful opportunity for me, Mama, for all of us. It will mean more money and a chance to write the stories myself. Then, maybe someday, I can write real books like Mark Twain or Charles Dickens."

Henrietta was having none of it. "Enough with this crazy talk of yours, Dexter." The conversation was over, for now. Later, when the time came to pack and get ready, reality would descend on her gradually, like a ray of sunshine through a cellar window. "Dinner is almost ready, so make yourself useful and go find your brother. He's probably outside playing."

Dexter stifled a snort. Harvey was outside, but make no mistake, at thirteen he was already past playing anything. No, most likely he was hanging out with his hoodlum friends, smoking cigarettes and drinking beer outside the poolhall. Harvey was another little bundle of bad news that Henrietta had yet to comprehend, despite the fact that he had dark nicotine stains on his fingers and sometimes reeked of beer, coming home drunk on more than one occasion.

Dexter trundled down the three flights of stairs and walked east to the corner of Court and Pacific Streets, past a bakery, a Chinese laundry, and Sweety's cigar store. Inside, Lester Sweety and Shing Tip Whoo, from the laundry, were playing checkers, sitting on wooden crates. Outside the shop was a real wooden Indian, nine feet tall. The Indian's face was painstakingly carved to make him look meaner than a thirty-year longshoreman. A red headdress adorned the top. The locals had tagged the wooden Indian Chief Sitting Duck, hardly a fitting name, Dexter mused, for such a noble creation.

"Maybe I'll be seeing you soon, Chief," Dexter said to him. He passed the wooden warrior twice a day at the very least and had never given him much thought one way or the other. Now, though, he felt something akin to awe and even respect, despite the lofty yarns he proofread each day, many chronicling deadly Indian attacks on wagon trains, where settlers had their hair lifted by tomahawks and had their eyelids sliced off and were smeared with honey and staked out on anthills.

"You wouldn't really scalp me, would you, Chief?" Dexter asked the hulking cigar store redskin. "I'm going to Texas, you see, and I would probably enjoy the trip a lot more if I didn't get killed. So you leave me alone and I'll leave you alone. Have we got a deal?"

A voice from behind him said, "If you're waiting for an answer, you got a very long wait."

Dexter turned to see Beinstock the fish peddler pushing his cart toward the corner. He was a short, squat little man with a massive salt-and-pepper beard that covered half his face. He always wore a black hat and black pants. Judging from the rotten smell of unsold mackerel and herring wafting from the pushcart, Beinstock was wisely about to call it a day.

"I don't suppose you'd know what kind of Indian he is, would you, Mr. Beinstock?" Dexter asked him.

"What kind?" Beinstock wiped his brow with a dirty rag. "The kind that stands there all day long and let's birds shit on his head, only he's made out of a tree so he's probably used to it. That's what kind of Indian he is."

"No, I meant what tribe," Dexter said.

"Tribe?" Beinstock stuffed the dirty rag into his back pocket. He studied the Indian for a second or two. He said, "I couldn't say, but I don't think it's mine."

Lester Sweety and Shing Tip Whoo had temporarily abandoned their game of checkers and were now listening in the doorway. Lester Sweety was a onetime bare-knuckles fighter and the terror of Cobble Hill, Brooklyn. Now, he was gray haired with a pot belly and had been selling candy, newspapers, and cigars since Dexter could remember. Shing Tip Whoo, a scrawny little Chinese man with a ponytail and funny hat, was likewise a neighborhood fixture.

"He's just an Indian, son," Lester Sweety said. "They're all the same, they're all redskins."

"Oh, no, Mr. Sweety," Dexter said. "They're not all the same. There's the Comanche and the Najavo and the Cheyenne Sioux and the Pawnee and the Shawnee and the Apache and the Choctaw and the Blackfeet." Dexter knew this from his work.

"Indians have black feet?" Shing Tip Whoo wanted to know.

"No, they have red feet," Sweety said. "They have red skin, like it says in the newspapers. What's wrong with that? Yours is yellow."

"How can their feet be black if the rest of them is red?" Beinstock asked now. "This I don't understand."

"Oh, that's just what they call themselves, their feet aren't really black," Dexter said, as if this alone would explain it. He turned to Mr. Sweety, "You haven't seen my brother Harvey around, have you?"

"There's a hot dice game down in the alley behind the police station." Sweety said. "You may want to check there first."

"Thank you, Mr. Sweety," Dexter said, and walked briskly toward the corner. Behind him he heard Beinstock say, "Red skin, black feet. Only in America."

The cries of winners and losers, along with the clattering of dice against cobblestone, flowed like smoke from the alleyway. Dexter rounded the corner and went into the alley. Aside from the uniformed policemen, it was initially hard to pick anyone out of the crowd, what with a dozen or so ruffians dressed in knickerbockers and heavy overcoats despite the warm weather.

Then Dexter spotted him. A runny-nosed boy with streaks of dirt down his face, and a cigarette hanging from the left corner of his mouth. He was arguing bitterly with a boy who was a good four inches taller and twenty-five pounds heavier. Dexter couldn't hear what the argument was about—money, no doubt—but before Dexter could get any closer, fists started flying, those of Harvey and his larger adversary. Harvey was immediately struck squarely on the nose and slammed back against the wall of the police station. Dexter's eyes widened as he saw the blood gushed from both of Harvey's nostrils.

By this time, the crap shooters had parted like the Red Sea to give the brawlers ample fighting room. Bets started coming down as to the victor, from cop and lawbreaker both.

Harvey was a scrapper. He pushed himself off from the wall, ignoring his crushed nose, and bounded back into the fray. He neatly ducked a roundhouse blow from the larger guy, spun, and hammered his opponent with a swift blow to the jaw. The thug's snapped back like a cap being wrenched off a bottle of soda pop. It was a nice solid punch, but for certain the last Harvey would throw before the other guy pounded him into a bloody pulp.

"Harvey!" Dexter cried.

The cops would be of no help. Only Dexter and Dexter alone could save his brother. He charged ahead into the crowd of bloodthirsty onlookers, but was quickly grabbed by beefy hands and hustled off to the side. He tried again to squeeze through the mass of bodies, and was again pushed to the back of the crowd. On his third attempt, Dexter was greeted by a burly cop with a boiled-potato face and the bushiest white eyebrows he'd ever seen on anything human. The cop grabbed Dexter by the frayed lapels of his suit coat and lifted him a good ten inches off the ground. "I got me two dollars on the big man, so stay the hell out of this laddie, or I'll kick ye till you're dead," he said, breathing whiskey fumes into Dexter's face.

"The little one," Dexter pleaded to the cop. "He's my brother." Harvey was losing ground now, vainly trying to shield himself from the big guy's blows.

"I don't care if he's yer sainted grandmither, be on yer way," the cop said, and hurled Dexter backward into the crowd.

He couldn't let his baby brother die. Dexter waded back into the sea of bodies and somehow managed to push his way through to the front lines.

His timing could not have been better—or worse, depending on perspective. He managed to grab Harvey and shove him out of the way just as Harvey's opponent was about to connect with a fierce blow. Instead, the punch took Dexter squarely on the chin.

Dexter stood for a heartbeat, looking more stunned than injured. His eyes crossed from the force of the punch, then rolled up into his head until only the whites were showing. He fell backward, stiffer than Sweety's cigar store Indian, right into Harvey's arms, out cold.

The next thing he remembered was coming awake as

Harvey splashed the dregs of a bucket of warm beer onto his face. It smelled something awful, but did the trick. Dexter sat up abruptly, sputtering rancid beer, and wiped his eyes. They were alone now, the crowd having scattered.

"The fight . . . Harvey . . ." Dexter gasped.

"The fight is over," Harvey said, flinging the bucket away. "We lost."

Harvey helped his older brother to his feet, saying angrily, "What'd you butt in for? I was just about to beat the bejeesus out of that peckerhead."

Dexter said groggily, "Yes, I could see how well you were doing."

"Whaddaya want here anyways, Dexter?" Harvey asked, still peeved that his brother had spoiled all the fun.

Dexter rubbed his swollen jaw and spit out some blood. The punch had split his lip against his bottom teeth.

"Dinner is ready," he said.

"I ain't hungry," Harvey said defiantly, and started walking away.

Dexter grabbed his arm and yanked him back. Harvey glared at him. Though five years younger, he stood only an inch shorter than Dexter. No longer was it possible to simply yell at Harvey to bring him into line like Dexter used to. Harvey was bigger now, not to mention bolder. It suddenly struck Dexter, seeing the hate and anger in his little brother's eyes, that Harvey might even be able to whip him royally in a fight. The thought chilled him.

"Harvey," Dexter said, "I'm your older brother and you have to listen to me."

"The hell I do," Harvey snapped, shaking loose of his brother's grip. "I'm thirteen years old and I don't need you. I don't need anybody, so piss off."

He started walking away again.

Dinner was eaten in sullen silence

Mr. Sweety had given Dexter and Harvey wet rags to

clean themselves up with. Harvey wolfed down his food; he was late for another crap game.

"Harvey," his mother said, "don't eat so fast. It's not good for the digestion."

Harvey reacted as he usually did—he ignored her. He grabbed the half-eaten veal chop and stood up, announcing, "I gotta go."

"But you haven't finished," Henrietta protested.

"C'mon, Ma," Harvey said. "I got things to do."

Henrietta stared at her son and mustered up as stern a voice as she could. "Harvey, you will sit and wait until we're all done."

Grumbling, Harvey sat back down. His mother continued, "And I won't have you running all over the streets after dark. Don't you have any homework?"

"I did it," Harvey said, annoyed.

Dexter snorted. Harvey hadn't done any homework since the third grade. Dexter was the one who usually ended up cracking Harvey's books for him. Harvey was going to have the college education Dexter never would, or Dexter would die trying.

"Mama," Dexter said, "have you thought any more about what we talked about? You know, about me going to Texas on Monday?"

"Texas?" Harvey asked. "Where the hell is Texas?"

Dexter said, "Maybe if you spent more time with your schoolbooks and less time in the billiard parlor you'd know where it is."

Harvey flung his veal chop across the table at his older brother, who neatly ducked. The veal chop sailed over his head and hit the wall with a splat, leaving a noticeable grease stain. Harvey cried, "Shut your piehole or you'll get the back of my hand!"

"That's enough, both of you," Henrietta said. "Why can't you boys get along?"

Dexter had had enough. He'd already taken a hefty

punch in the mouth for his ungrateful brother and now the little shit was hurling dinner at him. He bolted out of his chair and did the one thing that got Harvey's attention. He grabbed him by the ear and said, "You're coming with me, right now."

Clenching his brother's ear, Dexter, who could be assertive on rare occasions, escorted Harvey out of the apartment door and up the three flights of stairs to the rooftop. He pushed Harvey through the door and followed him out. The sun was a sinking fireball in the West. From the roof, they could see half of Brooklyn and most of the Lower East Side across the river in Manhattan.

Mr. Klapsattle, a German man who lived on the fourth floor, was on the roof tending to his pigeons. He had a big droopy moustache and wore red suspenders, standard attire for members of the South Brooklyn Fire Brigade.

"Goot evenink, Dexter, goot evenink, Harvey," Mr. Klapsattle greeted.

"Hello, Mr. Klapsattle," Dexter responded. He gave Harvey a little kick in the backside with his knee. "Where's your manners? Say hello."

"Hullo," Harvey said listlessly.

"Beautiful weather we had tomorrow," Klapsattle commented, stroking one of his dirty pigeons. Rumor in the neighborhood was that Klapsattle cooked and ate his birds from time to time, which explained why his dinner invitations were rarely accepted.

"Yes," Dexter replied with a smirk. "I hear yesterday's is supposed to be even nicer."

"What do you want?" Harvey asked his brother. "I got stuff to do, places to go."

"The only place you're going is back downstairs to Mama," Dexter said. "Starting Monday, you're going to be the man of the house."

"I am?" Harvey asked.

"That's right," Dexter said. "I'm going on a trip. A long

one, to a place that's farther away than I ever imagined—Texas, America."

"Where's that?"

"About two thousand miles as the crow flies," Dexter said, just as one of Mr. Klapsattle's pigeons flew the coop and dropped a big load an inch from where they stood. "Pigeons, too," he added. "I want you to take care of her while I'm gone," Dexter said. "That means staying out of pool halls, saloons, crap games, and fistfights. Think you can do that?"

"I guess so," Harvey said. "When are you coming back, Dexter?"

"I dunno," he replied. "Why? Think you'll miss me?"

"In a pig's ass," Harvey replied, but grinned a little bit.

"That's what I thought," Dexter said, and grinned back. "Come on, let's go downstairs. Mama made a nice angel food cake. We'll have some."

"Dexter?" Harvey asked. "Do you . . . do you remember Papa?"

It was an odd question to ask, but Dexter replied, "Yes, I remember him."

"Did he like me?"

"Yes, I guess he did," Dexter said. "Of course, when he was drinking, which was most of the time—I mean on those rare occasions he was home—he didn't like anybody very much. It's not like I could ever forget that look in his eyes when he was drunk and beat up on Mama. I see that same look in your eyes sometimes, Harvey. Why do you think we fight so much? I don't want to see you end up the way he did, all drunk and angry at the world."

Harvey seemed to comprehend this, but Dexter wasn't wholly convinced. He said, "You know I love Mama and all, but we both know she's a little . . . a little . . ."

"Empty-headed?" Harvey offered.

"That wasn't what I was looking for exactly," Dexter said, "but it'll do. Mama doesn't always see the world like

29

the rest of us do. I mean, she hears what she wants to hear and sees what she wants to see. With me gone, you'll have to take care of her, Harvey. And that means staying out of trouble. Because I'll tell you this: In a year, maybe two, you're going to be bigger and stronger than I am, and when that happens, you can beat the stuffing out of me. But until then, if you don't take good care of Mama, so help me God, Harvey, I will throw you out of this house and never let you come back. Do you understand?"

"I guess so," Harvey said.

"That'll have to do," Dexter said.

4

Fargo was holding three aces and a pair of queens. There wasn't any reason why he should be sweating, but he was. His armpits were leaking like too much milk in a goat's udders.

The drummer from Indiana, name of Casey, chewed on his cigar and considered the raise from Painless Hiram Quick, a short, ruddy-faced dentist who got his nickname by working on the good people of Paradise under the influence. "Hiram don't feel any pain when he yanks a tooth, but his patients sure as hell do," was the word around town.

There was over two hundred dollars on the table, at least seventy of it belonging to Fargo. The fourth player was Jedadiah Starkwell, the editor of the *Paradise Star Telegraph,* a notorious lush, but not a bad poker player.

The drummer from Indiana threw in his hand and spit on the floor. "Too rich for my blood," he said. Fargo remembered Casey saying he was an anvil salesman.

There was no way Starkwell or Hiram Quick could beat Fargo's hand. He silently begged for Jed Starkwell to stay in the game.

Jed Starkwell examined his cards through bleary eyes for the tenth time during the hand. He decided to stick around. He tossed some paper money into the pot and declared, "I stay."

It was up to Hiram Quick. The nervous little dentist matched Starkwell's bet and said, "I must be crazy, staying around as I do, but I confess that I'm a glutton for punish-

31

ment." He wiped his bald brow with a soiled handkerchief. "I'm in, gentlemen."

Fargo tried to suppress the chuckle that gurgled up his throat. He slapped down his cards, faceup, and said, "Aces over queens."

Jedadiah Starkwell grunted and tossed his cards down, grunting in disgust. "Poker, the devil's tool," he mumbled.

Fargo turned his gaze to Hiram Quick. The dentist smiled and wiped his brow. Fargo's heart sank. Quick laid his cards down, and damn if the sweaty little tooth-yanker didn't have four kings.

"I'm sorry, Mr. Fargo," Hiram Quick rasped, his beady black eyes flashing as he raked the cash into his sweat-stained derby. "To the victor goes the spoils."

Fargo wanted to spoil Quick with his fists, but that was poor sportsmanship. He poured himself another drink. He downed it in one gulp, turning his angry attention back to the sallow-faced, derby-hatted tinhorn who was sitting at the bar and staring at him, nursing a very flat beer.

"You'll excuse me, gentlemen," Painless Hiram Quick said, jamming the cash-filled hat onto his bald little head. A ten-dollar bill stuck out over his forehead. He scurried away from the table, taking the last of Fargo's money with him.

Jedadiah Starkwell rose from his chair and stood, a little shakily. He tipped his hat in Fargo's immediate vicinity and said, "Good-bye, Skye Fargo. You played hard and well. And on behalf of the citizens of Paradise, may I also extend our heartfelt thanks for the skillful way in which you dispatched the Danby brothers. A fine display of derring-do, Mr. Fargo, and of considerable journalistic interest to yours truly."

Fargo sipped his drink and said, "If it's all the same to you, Mr. Starkwell, I'd just as soon you not write about it."

"Pish posh," Starkwell said. "Why so modest, Mr. Fargo?"

"I got my reasons," Fargo said. "I'd be obliged if you didn't print nothing about me."

Starkwell shrugged and said, "As you wish, though it certainly is the biggest thing to hit town since that twister blew away half the town three years back."

With this, Starkwell staggered over to the bar for a nightcap—or a daycap, considering it was only two in the afternoon.

Fargo was broke. The reward money for the Danbys wouldn't be transferred to the Paradise bank for at least a week, he was told. It came from a group of ranchers up in the Territories. And the pasty-faced young guy wearing the derby was still sitting at the bar staring at him, checking him over like a San Angelo cattle trader.

Fargo had had enough. He stomped over to the pale stranger and said, "Who are you? Why are you watching me?"

The pale stranger tried to swallow. Finally he said, "I hope you're Skye Fargo."

"What if I ain't?"

"Then Mr. Huffington is going to be very angry," the pale young man said.

Fargo ordered a bottle and a dirty glass from the bartender, who brought both. Fargo poured himself a double shot of whiskey and raised the glass at the stranger.

"To your health," he said, then slammed the glass down onto the bar and poured out another. He pushed the glass over to the tinhorn and said, "Now you drink one to my health, stranger."

The young guy looked at the glass of whiskey and chewed his upper lip. He said, "Am I supposed to drink this?"

Fargo said, "You damn well better. Else I may be forced to kill you for staring at me."

The stranger looked at Fargo and saw the face of God.

He picked up the glass and looked at it as though it might bite him.

The stranger, whose age Fargo put at nineteen, twenty at best, swallowed half of the booze and tried not to look overwhelmed. His face turned a startling shade of purple. He started coughing violently, whiskey spurting from his nose and his eyes filling with tears.

Fargo said to the kid, "You made me lose, starin' at me and such."

The kid looked guilty. "I'm sorry, Mr. Fargo."

Fargo said, "Who are you? What do you want?"

The kid said, "My name is Dexter Tritt, and I've come a very long way to see you."

Fargo said, "I'm listening."

Dexter Tritt said, "Livermore and Beedle want you back, Mr. Fargo."

Fargo's eyes widened. He said, "Livermore and Beedle did you say?"

Dexter Tritt said, "Yes, sir."

Fargo turned and walked away, pushing through the batwing doors. He went out into the street, and walked toward his hotel.

Dexter Tritt ran after him, holding onto his derby and trying to keep up.

"I wish you would give me a minute of your time, Mr. Fargo," Dexter said. "I came all the way from Brooklyn, New York, sir, and it would mean—"

Fargo walked a little faster, Dexter trotting after him like a dog nipping at his heels.

Fargo said, "What did you say your name was again?"

"Tritt, Dexter Tritt," Dexter said.

"How old are you, Tritt?"

"Twenty-four," Dexter said.

Fargo stopped and looked at this Dexter Tritt. He was perspiring something fierce.

Fargo said, "How old?"

"Twenty-three," Dexter replied, though it sounded more like a question.

Fargo said, "How old?"

"Twenty-one next month," Dexter said.

"That's better," Fargo said, and started walking fast again. Dexter had to run to keep up.

"Mr. Fargo, if I could just—"

Fargo said, "Yonder at the end of this street is my hotel, Dexter Tritt. What I aim to do is go back to my room and sleep for about twelve hours, then when I wake up I'm gonna buy me the biggest breakfast Paradise has to offer: steak and eggs and bacon and flapjacks and lots of biscuits. I'll drink a pot of coffee and then light up the fattest, stinkiest cigar I can find. That's my plan, and you ain't a part of it. So do yourself a favor, boy. Get back on the next train goin' anywhere East and tell your people at Livermore and Beedle that Skye Fargo ain't for sale no more. You got that?"

Dexter Tritt, wide-eyed, said, "I can't do that, sir."

"Oh?"

"Mr. Huffington said that if I couldn't persuade you to come back to Livermore and Beedle, I shouldn't bother coming back at all."

"Did he now?" Fargo asked. "Am I that popular?"

"Oh, yes sir," Dexter said. "Popular and more. And to speak God's honest truth, sir, I really do need to keep my job."

Fargo kept walking. He said, "Do you now?"

Dexter nodded and said. "My mother and brother depend on me, yes sir they do. I can't go home until you agree to come back to Livermore and Beedle. Otherwise, we'll all starve. Jobs are hard to come by in New York, Mr. Fargo."

"Be that as it might," Fargo said, "you best get on back there, Mr. Tritt, 'cause I ain't gonna be changing my mind."

Fargo reached his hotel, the Diamond House, and took

35

Dexter's hand, shaking it. "A pleasure to meet you, Mr. Tritt. Welcome to Paradise, now go home. Believe me when I say, you may lose a job, but you'll live a lot longer if you get shut of me as soon as you can."

"Meaning what, Mr. Fargo?" Dexter Tritt wanted to know.

"Meaning people tend to find themselves dead when they latch onto me," Fargo said.

"I'm not sure I understand, Mr. Fargo," Dexter said.

Fargo raised his voice, "If you're from Livermore and Beedle you must have known Eddie Buzzell."

"Eddie Buzzell?" Dexter asked. It took him a minute before he remembered the name. "Sure, Eddie Buzzell. Mr. Huffington said he was the one who came to Texas and liked it so much he decided to stay forever."

Fargo looked disgusted. He said, "Yeah, Eddie stayed all right, but he didn't decide shit."

With that, Fargo disappeared into the hotel, his impossibly huge figure disappearing through the wooden door. Then, just as quickly, the door opened and Fargo stuck his head outside and said to Dexter, "You got yourself a place to sleep, boy?"

Dexter said, "Yes, thank you, Mr. Fargo."

"Where?" Fargo asked.

"Same place as you, Mr. Fargo," Dexter said. "Right here at the Diamond Hotel, room nine."

Fargo sighed tiredly and pulled the room key from his pocket. Engraved on it was a crude number ten.

"I hope you don't snore too loud, Dexter Tritt," Fargo mumbled with drunken exhaustion, " 'cause if you keep me awake, I'll kick you till you're dead."

5

Dexter sat on the hotel chair, his ear flat against the wall. In the next room, he could hear Skye Fargo snore, sputter, and fart in his sleep.

Dexter had been sitting in the same spot for about fifteen hours. It was a little after four in the morning. When Skye Fargo said he was going to sleep, he wasn't just clicking his teeth. The man truly knew how to grab forty or fifty winks.

Dexter had been fighting it himself, waking up and realizing that he had been asleep. Hardly a habit that any self-respecting storyteller could afford. He forced himself awake for the fifth time that night, only to hear more of Fargo's steady snoring.

When Dexter jerked awake, the sun was poking fat rays through the stiff window curtains six inches above the upper panes. He knew instinctively that it was nigh unto eight o'clock, maybe later.

Not good. Back in New York, Dexter remembered dimly, they were already proofreading the galleys for next week's installment of *Dandy Dan Candy, Prince of Pistoleers.* Not that anybody back in New York much cared that Dexter Tritt had his own new job to do, that job being Skye Fargo.

The mirror on the cigarette-scarred desk by the wall was covered with half an inch of prairie dust. Dexter wiped away a few square inches of the stuff and examined himself closely from the neck up. There was actually some dark

37

matter on his chin and cheeks that faintly resembled a beard. His brown hair was a greasy, tousled mess. Dexter smiled into the mirror, running his tongue over his front teeth, and felt almost a week's worth of crud.

Six days on just as many trains, usually without so much as clean drinking water, was taking its toll. Dexter felt like he hadn't had a decent night's sleep in years, not to mention anything that even remotely resembled real food. Greasy stew, moldy sandwiches, rotten fruit, and stale, bug-infested cakes seemed to be the best that any traveler could hope for south of St. Louis.

Dexter hiked up his pants once again. He'd lost some weight since embarking on this journey; he couldn't help but notice the dark patches under his eyes. He was thirsty all the time. Hungry, too, but thirsty even more. Either way, his stomach was making noises the likes of which Dexter hadn't thought humanly possible. Solid food was necessary, and soon.

Fargo. Dexter jammed his ear to the wall, but heard no snoring. Which meant Fargo was long gone.

Dexter didn't even bother changing his underwear. He bolted out the door and took the stairs three at a time down to the lobby. If Fargo left town, heaven forbid, or some other horrible fate took him, Dexter was as good as unemployed. Panic rose in his throat.

The hotel day man, a short, skinny fellow with thinning hair, name of Pendrake Roach, sat leaning against the wall behind the desk, snoring like a baby. Dexter slammed his hand down on the bell. Roach came awake with a snort and a grunt. "Mr. Tritt, what can I do for you?"

"Skye Fargo," Dexter said, out of breath. "Where is he?"

Roach blinked a few times and yawned. He said, "You know what time it is?"

Dexter didn't. He'd never owned a watch. He said, "No, I'm sorry I don't."

"No problem," Pendrake Roach said. He pulled a stopwatch from his vest pocket and gave it a quick glance. He said, "Ten after eight."

"Thank you," Dexter said.

"Anything else I can do for you, Mr. Tritt?" Roach asked.

Dexter was confused for a moment, then remembered. He said, "Mr. Fargo. Have you seen him?"

Roach nodded and said, "Came downstairs maybe half an hour ago. You might find him down at Toody's Café havin' his breakfast. That's usually where he is this time of the day."

"Thank you, Mr. Roach," Dexter said, and turned to leave.

Roach said, "That is, if he ain't hankerin' for either a drink or a woman first. Sometimes he does."

Dexter said, "And where would he find those, Mr. Roach?"

"Anywhere he wants," Roach replied, as if it was the most obvious thing in the world.

Fargo was lingering over his third cup of coffee, reading the *Paradise Star Telegraph* and rolling a smoke when he saw Dexter fly through the door. The kid was perspiring something terrible.

Fargo saw Dexter look around frantically until he spotted him with relief. Dexter made his way toward him, skirting the round tables occupied by hungry cowboys and local businessmen.

Dexter reached the table and respectfully took off his hat. Panting hard, he said, "I've been looking for you, Mr. Fargo."

"You found me."

"I've been to every saloon and house of ill . . . fallen women in town," Dexter said. He wiped his forehead with a dirty handkerchief.

"How'd you do?" Fargo asked.

"Not too well," Dexter said. "I didn't find you in any of them."

"Every now and then I like to take a meal," Fargo said. "Looks like you could use one yourself. Sit down, Dexter Tritt, and eat something."

Dexter sat.

"Lucille!" Fargo called out.

A short, squat basket of a woman tottered over to the table. She wore a dirty white apron and, like everything else in Texas, was covered with an inch of grit.

"The blue-plate special for our friend from New York," Fargo said to her. "Heavy on the beans."

"Don't look like he could hardly stand it, Skye," she said, eyeing Dexter suspiciously.

Fargo waved her away. "Off with you, bawdy wench, and bring this fair lad sustenance."

Lucille giggled like a schoolgirl and disappeared into the kitchen.

"Thought I told you to leave," Fargo said.

"And I believe I told you why I couldn't, sir," Dexter said. Fargo gently and carefully folded his newspaper, taking his time, then slammed it hard onto the table. His coffee cup bounced and a saltshaker fell over. Dexter flinched.

Fargo looked Dexter squarely in the eyes, his expression the meanest he could muster before his fourth cup of coffee.

"I told your half-wit bosses back in New York that our agreement was null and void," he said. "I ain't interested in sellin' my life to anyone, printed on cheap paper or otherwise. Not anymore."

"Mr. Fargo," Dexter said, "I just don't understand why all of a sudden, in the middle of a very successful publishing program, you changed your mind. The Skye Fargo stories are Livermore and Beedle's most profitable series."

"I got my reasons," Fargo said, "and they don't concern you or anyone else. I sent the money back, a banker's check

40

for three thousand dollars and some change. As far as I'm concerned, me and Livermore and Beedle are even."

Dexter reached into his wallet and started pawing clumsily through it. He said, "Uh, that's correct, Mr. Fargo. Three thousand, one hundred and twelve dollars. And sixteen cents." He kept searching through the wallet, not finding what he wanted. "Livermore and Beedle have authorized me . . . to return this check . . ."—he continued searching, having no luck—". . . to you herewith."

Dexter looked exasperated for a moment,—then seemed to remember something. He took off his left shoe and reached inside, pulling out a piece of paper.

He said, "I kept it in my shoe so I wouldn't lose it."

He handed it to Fargo. There was a gaping hole in the middle of it. Dexter examined the sole of his shoe. It too had a hole in it.

"Texas is very hard on shoes," Dexter said, grinning weakly. "But I'm sure the check is still good."

Fargo tore it into a dozen even, tiny pieces and tossed them over his shoulder.

"Not anymore it ain't," he said, and took a sip of coffee.

Lucille returned from the kitchen carrying a tray laden with breakfast. She set on the table in front of Dexter a huge platter of steak and eggs, followed by a basket of biscuits, a huge plate of beans, and a jar of marmalade, the only item that wasn't swimming in grease. The beans—and the steak and eggs, for that matter—had a slightly grayish color.

Dexter looked down at the food, any appetite he had long gone, and said to Lucille, "You don't have any poached eggs on toast, do you? I have a nervous stomach, you see, and I'm only supposed to eat bland foods."

"This ain't no fancy French bistro, mister," Lucille said. "What you see is what we got."

"And I'll make sure he eats every bite of it, Lucille," Fargo said. "Now how about some more java?"

41

Lucille trotted off to the kitchen. Fargo turned back to Dexter, "You want to be a Texan, you got to eat like one."

Dexter gingerly plucked a biscuit from the basket and knocked it against the wooden table. Not a crumb fell off.

"I really can't eat this," Dexter said.

Fargo slammed his fist on the table. "Eat it," he said in a gentle but stern voice.

Dexter did, shoveling the runny, undercooked eggs into his mouth. He grabbed the knife and tried to saw through the steak. What wasn't gristle was bone. He stabbed vainly at it, then thought better of it, and started on the beans. They tasted like laundry starch.

Dexter was halfway through them when a big, burly man with a walrus moustache and a weathered West Texas face came into the cafe. He wore a giant, sweat-stained cowboy hat and had a tin star pinned on a brown leather vest that seemed hopelessly small on a man so large.

"Mornin', Skye," he said.

"Morning, Edwin," Fargo said.

The man sat down at the table. Fargo said, "Had your breakfast, Edwin?"

"Yeah, thanks," he said. He looked at Dexter, who was forking beans into his craw at a furious pace. The man said, "Friend of yours, Skye?"

"Nah," Fargo said. "He's just passin' through."

Marshal Edwin Fix gave Dexter no more thought, and said to Fargo, "Percy Shelton over at the bank asked me to tell you the reward money come through half an hour ago. You claim it anytime you're of a mind to."

"I'll do that, Edwin, and thanks," Fargo said.

The marshal stood and said, "When you get a minute, Skye, stop by my office. We got some business to discuss concernin' the Danbys."

The marshal left to make his morning rounds. Fargo looked back at Dexter. "Edwin Fix, marshal here in Paradise. A good man as lawmen go." He looked the boy up and down and chuckled, "Enjoyin' your breakfast, Mr. Tritt?"

Dexter looked almost as gray as the beans. "Delicious," he mumbled. "Could you tell me something, Mr. Fargo?"

"What?"

"Where would a man go to throw up around here if he felt the need?" Dexter asked.

"There's a privvy out back," Fargo said. "Not feeling too good, are you?"

"Fine," Dexter squeaked. He threw down his napkin and bolted out of his chair, making a hasty exit into the alley.

Fargo gave him a few minutes to toss the café's breakfast, then tossed a silver dollar onto the table and followed Dexter outside.

Dexter hadn't quite made it to the privvy, instead he was emptying his stomach between two trash cans.

Fargo said to him, "If I can't convince you to go home, Tritt, maybe the food in Paradise will."

Dexter, on his knees, his head buried in a trash can, coughed and breathed in the smell of rotting eggshells and other pungent garbage, which brought on another fresh spell of puking.

"Go home, son, and do it today. Tell Livermore and Beedle that Skye Fargo ain't for sale no longer. Take care now."

Fargo walked away. Dexter was too sick to follow.

6

Percy Shelton was a tubby, balding, bespectacled little man with a gravelly voice—a banker to the core.

He said to Fargo, "The Cattleman's Protective Association in Mineral Springs has posted the reward money as promised. Three thousand dollars is a lot of money, Mr. Fargo, but I would say you earned every penny, ridding the territory of those evil Danby brothers as you did. How would you like your money, cash or banker's check?"

They were sitting in Shelton's cramped office at the Paradise Mercantile Trust.

Fargo said, "Actually, Mr. Shelton, I'd like to give the money to someone."

Shelton looked confused. "Give it to whom, Mr. Fargo?"

"Eddie Buzzell left a wife and two children, I believe," Fargo said. "Back in New York. I'd like her to have the money if it's all the same to you, Mr. Shelton. I was hoping you could arrange that for me."

"Eddie Buzzell was the gentleman who died the night you took down the Danbys, isn't that right?" Shelton asked.

Fargo nodded. He said, "That's right."

"As I said, Mr. Fargo," Shelton said, "Three thousand dollars is a lot of money. If you were to deposit those funds here at the bank, instead of giving it all away, you would earn enough interest to build yourself a nice little nest egg. I could arrange to send Mrs. Buzzell a monthly stipend!"

Fargo said, "I'd rather do it my way."

Shelton was sweating a lot. Bankers who sweated a lot made Fargo nervous.

Shelton said, "I wish you would reconsider, Mr. Fargo. At six percent, compounded quarterly—"

Fargo grabbed Shelton's nose between his thumb and forefinger and gave the little man's honker a firm squeeze. Shelton yelped in pain.

With his other hand, Fargo fished into his shirt pocket and produced a folded-up piece of paper. He tossed it onto the desk, still holding Shelton's nose.

"This is Mrs. Buzzell's address in Bayonne, New Jersey," Fargo said. "I want the three thousand wire-transferred into her account there if she has one. If she doesn't, then send the money to any bank in Bayonne under her name."

He gave Shelton's nose a little twist for good measure. Shelton whimpered.

Fargo said, "And I would be grateful if you would handle the transaction personally, Mr. Shelton."

With that, he released the little banker's nose. Fargo stood, jamming his hat on his head. "I'll be back later today for my receipt, Mr. Shelton. Thank you."

With that, Fargo left Percy Shelton moaning and checking his nose for any signs of blood.

Fargo walked out into the bright sunlight. Banks were much too dark for his liking. He stood on the plank boardwalk, trying to decide what he felt like doing next. He didn't want a drink, didn't want another meal so soon after breakfast, didn't quite feel like having a woman or playing a game of poker.

He decided to go back to the hotel and have a little nap. He was starting to like taking naps every now and then. The thought disturbed him somewhat. Naps were for old people, not him. But he still wanted one.

Edwin Fix poured Fargo a glass of whiskey, then poured one for himself.

He corked the bottle and slid it back into the open bottom drawer of his desk. They lifted their glasses and clinked.

"Luck," Fargo said.

"Luck," Edwin Fix said.

They drank. Fix took the bottle back out of the drawer—why did he even bother putting it away, Fargo wondered—and poured them each another.

Marshal Fix asked, "Any particular reason why you saw fit to damn near break Percy Shelton's nose, Skye?"

It was almost five in the afternoon. Fargo had slept nearly six hours. Surprising, since he'd grabbed a solid twelve hours the night before.

"He's a weasel," Fargo said, sipping Fix's whiskey. "And I didn't like his face."

"I don't like Shelton's face neither," Fix said, "but I don't go trying to rip parts of it off."

"I had my reasons, and they were good ones, Edwin," Fargo said.

"Percy Shelton is a pillar of the community and a member of the town council as well. If you hadn't killed some Danbys, you might be cooling your heels in one of my cells right now."

"Okay," Fargo said.

Fix poured them each a third whiskey. He said, "You're still a guest in this town, Fargo, and don't forget it."

"All right, Edwin," Fargo said, sipping whiskey. "I stand warned. I assume you asked me here for a reason, and not just to stare at my pretty face."

"You got that right," Fix said.

"Something about the Danbys," Fargo said.

Fix nodded. "You kilt two of 'em, Skye," he said. "But there's plenty more of 'em out there."

"I've heard that, too," Fargo said.

"A mean bunch, them Danbys," Fix said, leaning back in his chair. "Word is, a gang of 'em is on the move. They were spotted up around Texarkana. There's a good chance they're headed this way."

"Your information any good?" Fargo asked.

"As good as it gets," Fix replied.

Edwin Fix leaned back in his chair and puffed on his pipe. "Must be a couple hundred of them up in the hills back to Arkansas. And not just Danbys, neither. They got a passel of relations up there, like the Gribble and the Gorch clans, just as nasty too. Low-down, back-shootin', inbred shitbirds is what they are. That bunch, they been the scourge of the Ozarks for nigh on six generations, maybe more, cuttin' a wide swath of death and misery in their wake. Men, women, children—it don't make no matter to the Danbys. They'll cut you from neck to nuts and laugh about it later.

" 'Bout twenty years back, give or take, my brother Douglas was one of fifteen lawmen led a raid on 'em, up around Perryville. Poor bastards never had a chance. The Danbys bushwacked ever' last one of 'em. Slaughtered 'em like hogs. Was talk at one time about sendin' troops in there to weed 'em out, but nothin' much come of it. Wouldn't matter anyway. The Danbys'd just fade back into the hills where nobody could get to 'em."

Fargo had been hearing hair-raising tales of the fearsome Danby clan ever since he could remember, but had always chalked them up to the stuff of legend—some truth, but mostly myth. Edwin Fix, though, was not a man prone to exaggeration. When he spoke, it was from experience. Fargo continued listening.

"The Danbys don't take kindly to anyone killin' their kin," he said. "Some sorta twisted code of honor they got. They'll be hankering for revenge, Skye Fargo, and no mistake. Won't be no stoppin' 'em till they've avenged their dead brothers, even if it takes years."

Fargo rolled himself a smoke and struck a match on the

underside of his chair. He blew a puff and asked, "You think I should leave town, Edwin?"

"Let's put it another way," Fix said. "I fought the Comanche, almost got my scalp lifted by a band of Apache down around Sonora. I've tussled with some of the toughest hombres that ever drew a breath, down in Mexico when I was fightin' for old Maxi-millian. But I'll tell you this, Skye Fargo, and you listen up good: If I had them Danbys mad at me, you wouldn't see my coattails for the dust. If you're a wise man, you may want to take that trip to Paris, France, you've always dreamed about."

"I never dreamed about taking any trip to Paris, France," Fargo said.

"Then you may want to start," Fix said, and puffed his pipe.

Fargo took a sip of whiskey, trying to think. "And what if I did go to Paris, France, or London, England, or to China? What then? You're asking me to run, and for the rest of my days. I can't do that. I *won't* do that. What kind of man would I be?" He paused, then asked, "Texarkana, did you say?"

"That's the scuttlebutt," Fix said.

"What about Earl?" Fargo asked. "The Danbys will probably try to bust him out of jail first, won't they?"

Fix nodded and said, "That'd be my guess. I sent word to Horace Pinkley, up to Mineral Springs, to keep an eye out. Knowin' Horace, though, he probably won't believe it. Stubborn old cuss, that Pinkley. Don't believe nothing he cain't see with his own two eyes."

"If the Danbys do darken our doors," Fargo said, "they'll rip this town to pieces whether I hightail it out of here or not, ain't that right?"

"I've studied on that possibility," Fix said. "Sent word out to the Rangers Tuesday last."

"And if they don't get here in time?" Fargo asked.

"I'm prayin' they will," Fix responded.

"Like it or not, Edwin," Fargo said, "looks like you're gonna be needing me. Couldn't hurt to have another gun handy if push comes to shove."

"Then stay if you're of a mind to, Fargo," Fix said. "But pray them Danbys don't take you alive. It'll be the tortures of the damned and no mistakin' that."

"Fair enough," Fargo said.

A groan came from the one occupied jail cell. Fargo turned, "Got a customer, do you Edwin?"

"Yeah," Fix said, capping the whiskey bottle and sliding it back into his desk. "I believe you've met him."

Fargo stood and walked over to the cell. Laying on the cot was Dexter Tritt, curled up into a little ball, his face buried in a pillow. He'd looked better.

Fargo said to Fix, "What's he in for?"

"Barfing in public," the marshal replied. "I was just about to let him go."

"I'd be obliged if you put him on the first train East, Edwin," Fargo said. "He's sorta been gettin' in my hair."

Dexter sat up on the cot. He looked three shades worse than death. He wiped his mouth on his sleeve and said, "But not as much as I'm going to, Mr. Fargo, not by a mile in the country."

"That's 'not by a country mile'," Fargo said, "and just what the hell are you talking about?"

"I'd like to hear more about these Danby people," Dexter said. "And why you killed two of them and sent a third to the gallows. I think it would sell a million copies."

"Shit," Fargo muttered.

"This is getting better all the time," Dexter said.

With one hand, Fargo held Dexter Tritt by the seat of his pants; with the other, he held onto the collar of Dexter's brown jacket. He dragged the kid down Main Street toward the train station, not giving him the opportunity to talk, much less protest or otherwise complain.

He forcefully escorted Dexter to the depot and flung him down on a bench. He said, "Move one inch and I'll tear your tonsils out."

He vanished into the station and came out a minute later. He plucked Dexter's battered derby from his head and dropped a train ticket into it. He sat down on the bench next to Dexter.

"The train to Fort Worth is on time," Fargo said, "and you'll be on it, or my name ain't Skye Fargo."

"Oh, I have no doubt your name is Skye Fargo," Dexter said. "What I don't understand is why you have such animosity toward Livermore and Beedle. We've been aboveboard with you since the day you signed the publishing contract. Mr. Huffington said—"

"I'll have your goods shipped out tomorrow," Fargo said. "They'll arrive back in New York a day or two after you do. That aside, I don't want to hear jack-shit out of you. Train'll be here momentarily."

They waited in silence until the train chugged into the station. Fargo grabbed Dexter by the arm and dragged him onboard, depositing him in a seat.

Fargo said, "You got money for food?"

"I think so," Dexter said.

Fargo fished a bill out of his pocket and dropped it into Dexter's lap. He said, "You'll thank me for this someday, Dexter, I swear you will. Stick with me, and nothing but evil will befall you."

"Mr. Fargo—" Dexter said, and started to stand.

Fargo popped Dexter squarely on the chin, a solid if uninspired punch that nonetheless served its purpose. Dexter's head snapped back like a bottle of sarsaparilla, his derby knocked off. His eyes rolled up into his head and he collapsed into his seat, out colder than a hunk of ice.

Fargo picked up Dexter's derby hat and jammed it onto his head. He tucked the train ticket under the hat and made his way to the front of the car. He gave the conductor ten dollars and said, "Make sure that boy gets to Fort Worth."

"Yes, sir," the conductor said. He looked over at Dexter, who was slumped in the seat. "Asleep is he?"

"Yes," Fargo said. "Like a baby."

7

Billie Sue Sizemore was the daughter of an East Texas dirt farmer, name of Willard Sizemore. Billie Sue's mother had died when her only daughter was eleven years old. From that day on, Willard took his daughter, in the biblical sense, every night thereafter, usually when he had himself a snootful of corn liquor.

Billie Sue escaped the dirt farm when she was thirteen and had been whoring ever since, working her way West as each temperance society chased her from one town to the next. She liked Paradise; nobody judged her or tried to run her out of town or marry her off to any dim-witted cowboys.

At present, she worked in the employ of Denver Goldie's Goodtime Saloon and Happytime Emporium, the best Paradise had to offer.

Goldie wasn't half bad to work for, either. She only demanded a third of Billie Sue's tips, where most greedy madams usually demanded half and sometimes more.

Billie Sue watched as the tall man, Skye Fargo, made his twice-weekly entrance. He was famous of late for having killed two of the Danby brothers, sending the third to the gallows. She hadn't had him yet—he usually picked Ramona, a dusky brunette with Cajun blood. But Ramona was taken, and Billie Sue hoped Fargo would pick her.

"Skye Fargo, as I live and breathe," Denver Goldie said, a huge smile splitting her heavily made-up face. She threw her arms around him and gave him a big, wet kiss on the mouth, then gave his butt a playful squeeze for good measure. "Didn't expect you till tomorrow night."

"Some things a man can't control, Goldie," Fargo said. "Like when he gets the urge for a woman or when he's gonna die."

"I reckon," Goldie said, taking a silk hanky and wiping the lipstick off Fargo's mouth, "but as for dyin', the smart ones try and postpone it as long as possible."

"Guess you're right," Fargo said, making his way into the plush whorehouse parlor, where women of varying ages and sizes sat lazing around until the next customer.

"Where's Ramona?" Fargo asked.

"Sorry, Skye, but she's otherwise engaged," Denver Goldie said. "If I knew you were coming—"

Fargo felt a slight tinge of jealousy and hated it. He liked Ramona. He wanted Ramona. She was beautiful, with her smooth, dusky brown skin and legs that went halfway up to heaven. A smile that damn near made a man's heart melt like ice in August, titties so well-rounded with perfect nipples, just made for sucking into the wee hours of the morning.

But Ramona wasn't here. She should have been, but she wasn't. From the corner of his eye, Fargo could see a somewhat skinny, but still adorable little blonde filly clad in a nightie that covered barely enough for a man's imagination to make it worth his while.

Fargo looked her square in the face. The little pixie looked back and smiled. Fargo went and sat down on the velvet-covered couch next to her, with Denver Goldie following him and beaming approvingly.

"Billie Sue's one of my best gals," Denver Goldie said. "The daughter of a Virginia tobacco grower. Got the bluest blood flowing through her veins that—"

"Thank you, Goldie," Fargo said. "Nice to see you again."

Denver Goldie shut up and made herself scarce, scampering into the kitchen to yell at someone.

Fargo said, "I'm Skye Fargo."

"I know," Billie Sue said, trying to look seductive. She did nicely. Fargo was interested—at least, he tried to tell himself he was.

Fargo checked out her breasts and everything else below. He liked what he saw. "You really from Virginia?" he asked.

Billie Sue took Fargo's hand into her own and gave it a healthy squeeze. She said, "Does it matter?"

"Not really," Fargo said. "Not to me."

"Wanna go upstairs?" she asked.

Fargo did, but not with Billie Sue. He still wanted Ramona. He stood and made his way toward the staircase. He went up, four steps at a time.

Billie Sue cooed, "Wait for me, lover," and started following him up the stairs.

Fargo turned to her and said, "Set yourself back down, gal. This ain't our time."

Billie Sue looked hurt, but she went back to the couch and sat. He saw Denver Goldie come running over, then heard her say, "I should've known he had the crazies for Ramona, Goddamn it. I saw it in his eyes, I did. Shoulda—"

Fargo didn't wait to hear the rest. He went back up the stairs to the first landing and marched down the hallway to the third door on the left. He knew it well.

Fargo kicked the door open, not in the mood for bullshit of any kind, thank you very much. Splinters of wood flew all over the hallway as the door popped open and Fargo stepped inside.

Ramona was flat on her back, her arms and legs curled around some man whose ass was bigger than it should have been. The fat-assed man abruptly stopped pumping her, wheezing like a rusty gate.

Ramona turned her attention to the huge figure in the

busted doorway. The fat man from Fort Worth turned his head to look as well. He said, "I think you just busted into the wrong room, cowboy."

"Nope," Fargo said. "This is definitely the right one. Now leave," Fargo said, feeling incredibly pissed off for reasons he didn't quite understand.

"The hell I will," the potbellied man said, giving Fargo his meanest look. Stark naked, his gut sticking out halfway to Oklahoma Territory, it was hard to take him seriously. "I'm paid up till midnight."

Fargo reached into his pocket and grabbed ahold of some bills. He dropped them onto the man's belly and said, "Now you're even. Go home."

Denver Goldie and some of the girls appeared behind Fargo in the hallway. Denver Goldie bellowed, "You cut this shit out right now, Skye Fargo. I run a respectable house here and you got to follow the rules, and the biggest one is no kicking down any damn doors."

Fargo gently eased Denver Goldie out of the room, saying, "Whatever you say, Goldie, honey. Everything is under control."

"Sure as shit don't look like it to me," Denver Goldie protested.

"We're just having a nice pleasant little confab, is all," Fargo said, closing what was left of the door behind her. "You can go now."

"And don't think I ain't gonna charge you for that door, Skye Fargo," Denver Goldie said.

The big man scrambled to his feet, caring less that his manhood was shrinking back to nothing by the second. He roared, "I'll have you killed, you dumb peckerhead. You just—Skye Fargo, did you say?" He looked at Fargo and added, "That who you are? One who kilt the Danbys?"

"The Danbys, the Goddamn Danbys," Fargo said. "That's all anyone knows me for, that I killed those shitbird Danbys. People forget I'm also a very fucking nice person."

The Fort Worth cattleman looked into Fargo's cold, lake-blue eyes and saw something that made him not want to continue this fight. It was a look he himself once carried, when he was a younger man. Unfortunately, he wasn't that younger man today. He hopped around quickly, trying to squeeze into his long johns, and stayed around just long enough to collect his pants and shirt and boots. He jammed his hat onto his big head and said, "Nice meeting you, Fargo." He turned to Ramona and tipped his hat, saying, "You too, ma'am." He made his leave, as gracefully as he could under the unusual circumstances.

"I am so glad I'm not him right now," Fargo said.

Ramona, furious, barked at Fargo, "Damn you to hell, Fargo—Mr. Castleberry was a regular, every third Friday of the month, like clockwork. And you bitched it all up." She smacked him in the chest with her fist a couple of times, hard. She liked it, and started pummeling him with both fists. "Goldie's gonna shit little green apples over this, you neck-bowed dumbshit flimflammer."

Fargo grabbed her by the wrists and pushed her away. "Now don't say nothing I might take offense to, Ramona."

Trying to wriggle her way out of his grasp, Ramona said, "Listen to me, Skye Fargo. I'm on sale to the highest bidder, day and night. And if you have a problem with that, you got only two choices."

"And what would those be?" Fargo asked, still holding her wrists. Ramona tried to get free, but not very hard.

"You can pay me for our love," she said, falling into his arms, "or you can make an honest woman out of me. Me, I just can't have it both ways."

Fargo wrapped his arms around her. She smelled good. "I'm gonna give this some serious consideration. Just as soon as I deal with some little problems that just came up. There's these men, see, and they just got out of prison down in the Arizona Territory. Could be a week or two be-fore—"

Ramona slapped him hotly on his left cheek and said, "Shut up, peckerhead, and knock me a kiss."

Ramona looked into his piercing eyes. "Do you really love the hell out of me, Skye?"

"Does it matter?"

"It might. Does it matter to you?"

He was laying very comfortably atop her. Her warm arms were wrapped around his neck, drawing him down against her. He felt her plump nipples rubbing against his chest. Fargo felt a bead of sweat run down his nose and splash onto her lips.

She tasted his sweat and loved it. She licked her lips and couldn't help but start nibbling on his ear. Fargo liked it when she did that.

"What do you think?" he asked.

Ramona traced a finger down his body. "I'm not paid to think, Skye."

"I don't know much from love," Fargo began, "Denver Goldie has eight girls working for her, Ramona, but you're the one I pulled a fat-assed rancher off of."

She chuckled and pulled him closer.

"And he was paid till twelve," he added. "Earliest midnight of his life."

"Just love me, Skye," Ramona said.

"I thought you'd never ask."

Fargo kissed her deeply on the mouth, on the neck, and started working his way south. His pecker was stiffer than week-old hardtack.

He took one plump brown nipple into his mouth and started sucking on it like a newborn babe. Ramona writhed beneath him, running her fingers through his hair and guiding him to her other nipple. Her flesh was warm and sweet and peppery. Fargo sucked greedily on it, running his tongue back and forth slowly.

Ramona moaned, wrapping her long, smooth legs

57

around him and curling her arms across his back and jamming his face pleasantly into her breasts. Her passion was real now, as opposed to the act she put on for her customers.

Fargo made his way down to her belly, nuzzling it. He kissed her long legs, her feet—and realized he could wait no longer. He slid back on top of her and kissed her deeply, loving her good. Ramona responded in kind, nibbling his ear. She opened her legs and awaited him hungrily.

She cried out softly as Fargo entered her, rubbing her legs against his. He thrusted rhythmically, and Ramona met him halfway, biting her lower lip in ecstasy.

Fargo came fast and came hard, exploding deep inside her. Ramona held him tight, rubbing her plump titties against his chest. He slammed his hips into her one last time and held on for dear life. It had been a long time since he'd made love to a woman he cared something for, and that seemed to make all the difference.

Fargo relaxed atop her and gave her another big kiss. She responded dutifully, kissing him back. Ramona was a whore and no mistake, but her affection for Fargo was genuine.

He rolled off of her and fought off the immediate desire to slip into slumber. He scooped her up so that they were clenched tightly together. After a few moments, Ramona said, "Do you really like me, Skye?"

He whispered, "I like you a lot, Ramona."

"Enough to make an honest woman out of me?"

Fargo said nothing, and his silence spoke volumes. He buried his face in her neck and planted little kisses there.

She said, "You came quick tonight, Skye. Something on your mind?"

Fargo tried not to think about the two remaining Danby brothers, and whatever prairie trash desperados they could pick up along the way, coming to Paradise to pay him a visit. The consequences could be dire. Still, he was determined not to let his worries interfere with his lovemaking. Life was too short.

With that, he felt himself becoming hard again. He said, kissing her, "Don't worry, baby. The train'll be back in the station anytime now."

"I'll be waiting," Ramona said.

8

Dexter took a deep breath and walked up to the bartender. "Excuse me, but could you tell me where I could find Mr. Skye Fargo?"

The bartender had a huge handlebar moustache. He spit into a filthy rag and started wiping the wooden bar with it. "Don't rightly know the name," he said.

"He's a tall man," Dexter said. "Six feet and several inches at least. He's got a scruffy beard, walks around in buckskins, and his boots are old and dusty, exactly the way the writers described him: tall, brooding, a loner who lives by his wits and guile and—"

"Like I said," the bartender interrupted, "I don't think I've made the man's acquaintance. You want another drink or what?"

Dexter looked at his glass. It was still full of whiskey. He was standing in a place called Hearn's Saloon, run by a foul-tempered little man with a nasty disposition who he assumed was Mr. Sneed Hearn, Prop., as the rotted little wooden sign hanging over the entrance proclaimed.

"I haven't finished what you already gave me, thank you," Dexter said.

"Well fine," Sneed Hearn replied, cocking an angry eyebrow at Dexter before making his way down the bar to a tall, leathery old cuss wearing an overcoat much too warm for the North Texas climes. Hearn poured the new customer a drink.

Dexter picked up the glass of whiskey and stared into it,

gazing into the thin brown liquid. He would no sooner drink this stuff than bathe in it.

An old, white-bearded stranger bellied up to the bar and slammed an empty beer mug down. He had at best three teeth in his mouth and a gut that stretched from here to tomorrow. "Hearn," he cried out, "another beer."

Sneed Hearn eventually got around to drawing the old geezer a beer, filling the mug and testily slamming it down in front of him, spilling half of it. "Drink this and leave me in peace, old man. And if ye ain't got the nickel to pay for it, you'll be cleanin' the spittoon come morning."

The white-bearded old man took a long drink of beer, wiped his mouth, then let loose with a belch that was loud enough to shake the heavens.

"What's the matter, son?" he asked Dexter, "Don't like Sneed Hearn's rotgut? Not that I blame you much."

"I'm not much of a drinker. I wouldn't know good whiskey from bad."

"They say tasting it is the real test," White Beard slurred, then picked up Dexter's glass and downed the whiskey in one gulp.

"Not bad." He put the shot glass down and said, "Now look what I've gone and did. I drank all your whiskey. Mr. Hearn, another for my friend here."

Sneed Hearn poured Dexter another. White Beard grabbed Hearn's wrist and said, "What's your rush, brother Hearn? Me and my friend here is working up a roarin' thirst."

Hearn knew better. "Who's paying, Buzzy?" he asked.

They both looked at Dexter, who put some money onto the bar. Hearn snatched it up. White Beard said, "And another glass if you'd be so kind, Sneed."

Sneed put another glass on the bar and went to wait on another customer as Dexter called out behind him, "I need a receipt, please Mr. Hearn."

White Beard poured them each a drink and said,

"Name's Oathammer, Buzzy Oathammer." He stuck his hand out.

Dexter took it and introduced himself.

Buzzy downed the whiskey in one gulp and said, "Ain't from around here, are you, Mr. Tritt?"

Dexter shook his head. "Brooklyn, New York," he said.

"New York," Buzzy said, having another drink. Dexter merely sniffed his. "There's a place I always wanted to visit. I hear tell it smells like fish."

"Only sometimes," Dexter said.

"What brings you to our fair little town, Mr. Trott?"

"Tritt," Dexter said, and proceeded to tell Buzzy Oathammer just that. As he did, Buzzy drained most of the bottle. It seemed to have little effect on him. When Dexter was finished, Buzzy said, "Skye Fargo? Sure, I know the man. Everyone knows Skye Fargo. He's a hero."

"So I've been hearing," Dexter said, and this time poured Buzzy a drink. "Something about the Danby brothers."

"Sure," Buzzy said. "Kicked their bushwackin' butts right into the middle of next week, Fargo did."

"Tell me all about it," Dexter said, pulling a writing tablet and a pencil from his briefcase. He started scribbling furiously as Buzzy described Fargo's exploits. Somewhere along the line, Buzzy had signaled for another bottle, which Sneed Hearn dutifully brought over. So caught up was Dexter in Buzzy's storytelling, he handed over the money to Hearn and didn't even ask for a receipt.

"Then they got the drop on Skye Fargo," Buzzy finished, getting drunker by the minute. "Fargo dropped and hit the ground firing, ventilating them five Danby boys—"

"Excuse me, Mr. Oathammer," Dexter interrupted, "but I heard there were only three Danby brothers."

Buzzy took another drink and said, "Hell's bells, son. When it comes to the Danbys, three's as bad as five!"

Dexter got it all. His cheeks were flushed and sweat was

beading on his forehead. Buzzy Oathammer had never seen a man so excited about anything not related to drinking or screwing. He finished telling the yarn.

"This is simply incredible," Dexter said giddily, dotting a couple of *I*'s and crossing the last of the *T*'s. "They say truth is stranger than fiction, and this certainly proves it." He took Buzzy's hand and pumped it. "I'd like to thank you for your time and cooperation. If you're ever in New York City and need a good home-cooked meal—"

The batwing doors flew open and two impossibly over-sized men burst in like twin tornadoes. They seemed larger than life, covered in prairie dust from hats to boots, spurs jangling like bells. They were bearded and burly and be-tween them were missing an eye, one and a half ears, half a nose, and a couple of fingers. A number of scars and stitch marks decorated their hairy faces.

A large space opened up at the bar as the two giants bel-lied up, a couple of Kansas City drummers scurried out of the way. One of them slammed his fist down, and Dexter could feel the vibration halfway down the wooden bar.

Dexter was riveted, unable to avert his gaze from the ru-ined faces of these massive men of the West. He barely no-ticed a tall, thin bearded man down at the far end of the bar who was quietly sipping a glass of amber liquid. The stranger was well-dressed, in a shiny new black suit and black boots. He seemed immune to the wave of fear that swept over the premises, his hat low on his forehead.

"Whiskey, you scurvy little piece of puke," the fist-banger thundered. Dexter never saw anyone move as quickly as Sneed Hearn. The ratty little saloonkeeper tended to the big men pronto, setting two bottles of whiskey in front of them and quickly making himself scarce.

Dexter couldn't help but gasp as the other man whipped off his hat and revealed a head that was sorely missing a scalp, sporting instead a hideous, scar-streaked dome that made him look something less than human.

Dexter gasped out loud. Buzzy Oathammer whispered into his ear, "Name's Stuckey McGee. Had his scalp lifted by some Mescalero Apaches down in Mexico some years back."

The big brute wiped his forehead with a dusty sleeve and jammed the hat back onto his head. The two big men lifted their bottles simultaneously and drank, their Adam's apples bobbing as the rotgut poured down their throats.

"Other one's Alvin Crimp," Dexter heard Buzzy mutter. "Bounty hunters. Sidewindin', back-shootin' scurvy low-life devils, worse than the men they track down."

Alvin Crimp finished the contents of his bottle and hurled it across the saloon, where it smashed against the piano. The piano player was long gone, having smartly taken refuge elsewhere. Stuckey McGee likewise downed the rest of his bottle and seemed no worse for the wear. Sneed Hearn appeared from the shadows and placed two more bottles onto the bar. This time he waited, giving his guests the eye until Alvin Crimp slammed a couple of silver dollars down.

"Take your money and go, ratface, or I'll know the reason why," Alvin Crimp growled.

Sneed Hearn quickly scooped up the money and wisely faded back into the shadows as Crimp and McGee went about some serious drinking. Dexter watched, transfixed. This was the real West, the one he'd only read about in the slew of dime novels he slogged through on any given day. And these men were the genuine article, as Mr. Huffington might say.

"Jesus God, but those are big men," Dexter said.

"That they are," Buzzy said. "And as mean as they are ugly."

Dexter's brain was working overtime. "I could get a ten-book series out of these guys. Maybe more," he said.

"Huh?" Buzzy asked, but too late. Dexter was already walking toward them. Buzzy reached out and deftly grabbed Dexter's arm, pulling him back.

"Where do you think you're going, boy?" Buzzy wanted to know.

"To talk to those men," Dexter said. "Livermore and Beedle are paying me to seek out new story ideas, and these men might just—"

Buzzy said, "Ain't a good idear. Them boys are capable of anything. They—"

Dexter was gone, making his way down the bar toward Crimp and McGee, who were busy drinking and yarning with each other. The saloon was deathly quiet save for their raucous laughter and dusty backslapping.

Dexter approached them and timidly tapped Stuckey McGee on the shoulder. The tall man seemed hardly to notice. Dexter tapped his shoulder again, harder this time.

At the other end of the bar, Buzzy Oathammer took a big swallow of whiskey and said a silent prayer for this dumb Easterner.

McGee stopped laughing and slowly swiveled his head to look at his shoulder. He saw some pale-faced, derby-hatted skinny weasel looking up at him.

The skinny kid said, "May I be permitted to discuss a serious business matter with you, Mr. McGee." Dexter added, to Stuckey Crimp, "And you as well, Mr. Crimp?"

Stuckey McGee looked down at Dexter, his expression more one of idle curiosity than blood lust. Dexter gazed up into Stuckey McGee's lifeless black eyes and suddenly felt a chill.

Their expressions were blank, devoid of any emotion or thought, as if Dexter was merely a water bug on the floor, there to be stepped on and forgotten.

He started talking faster, his armpits sweating. "I represent Livermore and Beedle Publications in New York City, and we publish a series of Western pulps and dime novels.

and maybe you've read and enjoyed some of our distinguished magazines and books or maybe you haven't. In any event I would be interested in discussing with you gentlemen"—He was babbling now, just like the cross-eyed idiot kid, Nathan Botts, who sat all day on an apple crate in front of Fanelli's Market on DeKalb Avenue and played with his toes—"at your earliest convenience, of course, and another time and another place or whatever, the possibility of creating a new series featuring your exploits with the Indians and I really wish one of you would say something because I'm running out of words, so I'll just back away now and let you gentlemen drink in peace because I'm a peaceable man, really, and far be it from me to—"

Finally, Artie Crimp spit a huge black wad of tobacco juice right onto the lapel of Dexter's suit jacket. It dripped down his pants and onto his shoes.

Dexter looked around briefly, and saw everyone in the saloon staring at him—except for the tall stranger at the end of the bar, who moved not an inch and might have been sleeping standing up.

Dexter had just been issued a challenge of some kind, he knew, but it would be certain death to respond. He started to back away slowly, not taking his eyes off Crimp and McGee, who looked back at Dexter with the same expression they might give a pesky horsefly.

It looked for a moment that Dexter might actually make it back to Buzzy Oathammer in one piece. Unfortunately, he bumped into a tall, trail-weary cowboy and stepped solidly on his foot. The cowboy yelped and pushed Dexter away roughly, snapping angrily, "Back off, dingleberry."

Dexter careened forward and crashed into the bar, flailing his arms uselessly, neatly managing to knock Alvin Crimp's bottle of rotgut onto the floor. It shattered at his feet, spraying cheap whiskey all over his pants.

Even still, Crimp didn't look mad, exactly, save for his

eyes, which were blazing with raw fury. He stood stock still, a gnarly old oak tree with red eyes.

"You broke my whiskey," Crimp said.

Dexter's lower lip quivered and he couldn't stop blinking. He stammered, "I don't suppose saying I'm sorry would help very much at this point, would it?"

Crimp plucked the jagged end of the broken bottle by the neck and waved it in Dexter's face. With his other hand, he grabbed Dexter by the shirt collar and lifted him a couple of feet off the floor. It took little or no effort.

Crimp said, "I'm a-gonna cut your heart out with this and feed it to my dawg, peckerwood."

Dexter's face turned the color of fresh milk and his eyes showed more white than eyeball.

He gulped and said, "Maybe I can come back another time, Mr. Crimp."

Buzzy Oathammer chose that advantageous moment to turn his head away and shut his eyes. Half a second later he heard a crash, followed by a wail of pain from his new friend.

"Oh, yes, Skye, my beautiful Skye, my sweet little Skye boy," Ramona moaned, riding Fargo now, straddling him. Fargo was rubbing Ramona's plump, shapely breasts as she raked her long fingernails across his bare chest. His ass was thumping up and down against the bed as she slammed her hips down, engulfing his manhood.

He sat up, his stiff pecker still deeply inside her, and wrapped his arms around her.

He kissed her, sliding his tongue into her mouth. Ramona responded in kind, their mouths glued together.

"Oh, Skye . . ." Ramona cried out in ecstasy, rubbing her titties in his face. He kissed them and sucked on her nipples. Damn, but he just couldn't get enough of her. "Say you love me."

"You love me," Fargo responded.

She ran her fingers through his tousled hair, pressing his face into her left tit. "No, my darling Skye," she cooed. "Tell me you'll love me forever and ever."

"Ramona, baby," Fargo said, "why the hell not?"

Fargo was ten seconds shy of exploding inside her, pumping furiously and floating on a sensual cloud of love, when the door flew open with a loud crack. Fargo, wrapped up totally in carnal bliss, didn't even notice until Ramona screamed and tumbled off him, scampering under the covers.

In the dim light of the hallway, Fargo saw Buzzy Oathammer, the town character, looming large in the shadows. Denver Goldie was trailing him as he stepped into the room.

Buzzy Oathammer said, ignoring Ramona completely but not forgetting to take off his rumpled hat, "Mr. Fargo, we need to go, and right quick."

"I'm sorry, Skye," Denver Goldie said, all flustered. "I told him you weren't to be disturbed, but he pushed past me and—"

"This better be good," Fargo said, " 'Cause if it ain't, some new assholes are gonna be ripped."

"Dexter Tritt," Buzzy said, all out of breath and perspiring. "Friend of yours, ain't he?"

Fargo had a sinking feeling. Not a second employee of Livermore and Beedle dead, not now. "What about him?"

"Alvin Crimp and Stuckey McGee are ripping *him* a new asshole over to Sneed Hearn's place," Buzzy said. "You best come quick afore they kill him till he's dead."

"Shit," Fargo said, scrambling for his pants. He buttoned them up and threw on his shirt. "I put that boy on a train headed East. How in hell did he get back here so friggin' fast?"

"Can't say," Buzzy said, "but he's back, and about to die one horrible death."

Fargo slid into his boots and grabbed his gunbelt from

the bedpost. He started to follow Buzzy out the door, then remembered something. He went to the bed and gave Ramona a nice big kiss and chucked a couple of silver dollars onto the bed.

"I'll see you later, girl," he said to her.

He was out the door before Ramona could even respond. She pulled the blankets more securely around herself.

Denver Goldie said, "I think he really likes you, Ramona honey."

Ramona plucked the silver dollars from the blanket and clenched them in her fist.

"Yeah," she said, sounding a trifle tired. She tossed the money into the corner of the tiny room, where they clinked melodically. "Here's to love."

9

One of the last things Dexter could remember was being turned upside down—Stuckey McGee taking one leg, Alvin Crimp the other—then feeling his head being jammed through wood and wires. Actually, he also remembered that it hurt like a son of a bitch.

Alvin Crimp had flung him effortlessly across the room, where he'd landed against the piano. Dexter felt a very sharp pain against his spine, then saw some amazingly beautiful stars in his head. He had passed out long before Stuckey McGee took a metal-studded whip to him, flogging him mercilessly. Alvin Crimp was content to kick Dexter in the ribs and face with the hard tip of his left boot.

Dexter vaguely recalled a couple of teeth being kicked loose and trying to sneak down his throat. He coughed and spit out a back molar. He drifted away again and sort of came to moments later, finding himself hanging upside down as sharp ribbons of wire, and wooden splinters tore painfully at his face.

What a stupid way to die, Dexter thought dimly. Then he went away and didn't come back for a while.

Fargo's first thought upon entering Sneed Hearn's saloon was, they're trying to stuff the poor bastard into the piano.

This was the sight that greeted him as he pushed through the batwing doors. Alvin Crimp and Stuckey McGee, two of the meanest bastards who ever drew the Lord's breath, were ramming Dexter, headfirst, into the guts of the piano. The player was huddled in a corner, his hiding spot uncovered by the ruckus, and made no move to reclaim the box of ivories, which was now damaged beyond repair and would never tinkle another tune.

Dexter's head was a blood-streaked disaster wrapped in wire and small chunks of wood. The big boys were having some serious fun with him, dunking him up and down, each of them holding a leg.

"Spill whiskey on me, will ya?" Crimp bellowed, and shoved Dexter into the piano even harder.

"Give 'im what fer, the little weasel," Stuckey McGee cackled.

Alvin Crimp yanked Dexter out of the ruined piano and grabbed him by the seat of the pants with one hand and by the collar with the other, raising him over his head. He was about to hurl Dexter straight into the middle of next week when Fargo pulled the Colt from his holster and squeezed off two shots into the roof.

At the sound of the gunfire, Alvin Crimp froze, Dexter still suspended above him.

"Fun's over, Crimp," Fargo said, aiming straight at Crimp's heart. "Put him down."

Fargo saw Stuckey McGee's hand drop and try to clear leather. Fargo pumped two bullets into his face, one above the left eye and the second into his lower jaw. Everything below McGee's nose vaporized into a spray of blood, tooth, and bone. He dropped like a sack of brass doorknobs.

Alvin Crimp released his grip. Dexter crashed to the floor with a thud that kicked up a small cloud of trail dust. Fargo felt an uncharacteristic tinge of affection for him. He was still a kid, really, trying to do a man's job, though with more enthusiasm than was obviously healthy.

Fargo said to Alvin Crimp, "You'd be wise to crawl back into whatever rathole you call home, and right quick."

He turned to Dexter and started to say, "I'd ask if you're all right, kid, but I don't hardly see the need—"

Fargo instinctively sensed some activity from Alvin Crimp. He moved to clear leather, but knew he was dead. He saw the glint of the knife blade, but too late. Crimp was clutching the knife chest-high, half a beat from flinging it deep into Fargo's belly.

Somewhere behind Fargo, a shot rang out. A bloody hole opened in Crimp's face. Stunned, the knife slipped out of his hand and clattered to the floor. He still stood—he was dead from the neck up, but the rest of him had yet to get the message. Fargo gently prodded Crimp with the tip of his forefinger. Crimp pitched over backward and crashed flat on his back, most certainly dead all over.

Fargo turned slowly and saw a tall, thin bearded man in black wielding a new model Colt. He didn't holster it right away. "It's my sincere hope that shot wasn't meant for me," Fargo said.

"You shouldn't worry," the bearded man said. He holstered the Colt. "I just don't like knives. Such a mess they make."

The man had a slight accent of unknown origin; his English sounded a little funny. Not that Fargo was apt to complain. It wasn't every day a tall man in black saved your life.

"You saved my bacon and I thank you kindly," Fargo said. "You mind if I ask why?"

The stranger looked down at Dexter and said to Fargo, "Your friend doesn't look very well. You maybe have a decent doctor in this crazy Texas?"

"Yeah, we got one," Fargo said.

Dexter moaned a little. Buzzy crouched down next to him and slapped Dexter's bloody cheek a couple of times to bring him around. Dexter didn't respond. Fargo grabbed a bucket of dirty mop water next to the bar and flung the contents into Dexter's face. His eyes fluttered open, blood running into them. Sneed Hearn rushed over, offering a damp bar rag. Fargo took it and dabbed it at Dexter's face, which was crisscrossed with angry red slashes.

He slid an arm under Dexter and raised him up into a sitting position.

Dexter grinned weakly and said, with some effort, "Hello, Mr. Fargo."

"I could've swore I put you on the train my ownself," Fargo said. "What the hell are you doing back here?"

"I couldn't leave without finishing what I came here to do," Dexter said, blood trickling from the corner of his mouth and running down his cheek. "Mr. Huffington wouldn't like it."

"I'd say you've just earned yourself a raise, son," Fargo said.

He and Buzzy hoisted Dexter up, where his head rolled from side to side. He was a bloody hash.

As they carried him out, Fargo said to the stranger, "Can I buy you a drink before I go?"

"A drink would be a niceness," the stranger said.

"Mr. Hearn," Fargo said to the saloonkeeper, "A bottle of your finest rotgut for the man, please."

"Yes, sir," Hearn said, and reached for a bottle of his pricier private stock. He poured the stranger a healthy dollop into a clean glass.

"You got a name?" Fargo asked the stranger. "Since you already seem to know mine."

"Oh, yes, I have a name," the stranger said, then lifted his glass of whiskey and said, "*L'chaim*, paleface." He knocked back the whiskey. Sneed Hearn poured him another.

"What did he say?" Buzzy asked.

Fargo shrugged. He said to the stranger, "Thanks again. I'll see you around."

"Of that I'm certain, Mr. Fargo," the stranger said, and sipped his drink. "It's God's will."

*   *   *

Fargo and Buzzy Oathammer dragged Dexter over to Emily "Ma" Fisher's boarding house. The Widow Fisher ran a nice quiet, clean place on the far end of town where her boarders went their own way and nobody asked any questions. The perfect spot for Dexter Tritt to heal, and healing was definitely in order.

Ma Fisher greeted them at the door, holding a lantern. "Shit on fire and save the matches!" she exclaimed after taking one look at Dexter. Fargo and Buzzy carried a bloodied Dexter into the foyer, as Ma Fisher rambled on. "This your doing, Mr. Fargo?" Ma was a stout, sixtyish woman with her gray hair tied, at this late hour, into pigtails. She had the energy of a woman half her age.

"For a change, no," Fargo said.

"Bring him upstairs," Ma Fisher said.

Fargo and Buzzy hauled Dexter up the steps. Ma Fisher bellowed, "Prudie, go fetch Doc Phipps, and make it snappy."

A young girl of no more than seventeen, her black hair also tied into pigtails, materialized at the bottom of the stairs. Fargo stole a glance at her immediately, noticing that she was shapely even under her bulky nightclothes, and cuter than a bug's ear.

She looked concerned, but not alarmed. "What if he ain't sober, Mama?"

Ma Fisher snapped, "Don't argue with me, girl."

"Yes, Mama," Prudie said, and dashed out the door.

They trundled Dexter up the stairs, Ma Fisher leading the way down the hall into a small but tidy bedroom. Fargo and Buzzy dropped Dexter onto the bed as Ma Fisher lit the lamp.

"I'll fix some coffee," she said, before making a hasty exit.

Fargo and Buzzy stared down at what was left of Dexter Tritt. "Think he's a-gonna make it?" Buzzy asked.

74

Fargo popped a cigarette into his mouth and struck a match against the wall. "He damn well better." Fargo took a puff and turned to the grizzled old coot. "Do I know you?"

"I'm Buzzy Oathammer," Buzzy said, sticking out his hand. "I work over at the stable, shoveling horsesh—doing this and that. I've been looking after your Ovaro."

"How'd you know where to find me?"

Buzzy shrugged. He said, "I might be just a stable bum, but I'm not as dumb as you look."

While Fargo chewed that one over, Ma Fisher came in carrying a tray. On it was a huge mug of steaming hot coffee, strongly laced with a healthy dollop of blackberry brandy. She set the tray down on the night table next to the bed.

"Sit him up," she said. Ma Fisher was a model of crisp efficiency.

Fargo and Buzzy got Dexter into a sitting position against the headboard. His head lolled from side to side as he slipped in and out of consciousness, more out than in. Even in the dim lamplight, his face was an unholy mess, looking much like the route map for the Union Pacific Railroad.

Ma Fisher tried pouring some of the coffee down Dexter's throat. Most of it came right back up, but she persevered. When the brandy hit his belly, Dexter coughed and sputtered, but rejoined the living. Ma took the opportunity to force more of the coffee into him.

Fargo sat on the edge of the bed. "You okay, boy?"

"I've felt better," Dexter responded. Every inch of his body felt on fire. Even blinking seemed a new adventure in pain.

"Looked better, too, would be my guess," Buzzy put in.

Ma Fisher hushed them, her attention focused on Dexter. "Don't talk, son, just drink."

She forced more coffee down his throat. The brandy started to have an effect. Dexter felt suddenly light-headed, much the same way he had when Mr. Huffington plied him with gin on that Friday afternoon that now seemed like years and years ago.

Downstairs, the front door opened and closed with a slam, and footsteps—two sets, it sounded like—came bounding up the stairs. Prudie Fisher came into the room, followed by a tall, gaunt man carrying a black bag. He wore a black hat and a rumpled gray suit and seemed a trifle unsteady on his feet.

"Over there, Doctor," Prudie said.

Doc Phipps made his way unsteadily over to where Ma Fisher sat on a chair next to the bed, still giving Dexter the coffee. He dropped his doctor's bag on the bed and said to Ma Fisher, his speech somewhat slurred, "All right, Emily, kindly remove all your clothes so's I can examine you."

Prudie Fisher giggled. Ma Fisher snapped, "I ain't the patient, you damn drunken fool. It's him, there on the bed."

She picked up the lamp and held it close to Dexter so that Doc Phipps could get a better look.

He did, and commented, "Sweet Jesus, this man needs a doctor."

Ma Fisher pulled the lamp away from Dexter's face and set it back down on the night table. "I better make more coffee. Mr. Fargo, you and your friend walk the good Doctor Phipps around the room for a spell so he can sober up some." "Come, Prudie," she added, to her pretty daughter. "There'll be no more sleep for us this night. Might as well start breakfast."

Doc Phipps collapsed into the chair and immediately started snoring.

"You heard the woman," Fargo said, and grabbed Doc Phipps's left arm. Buzzy scowled, and grabbed the right. Together they hoisted the pickled sawbones to his feet and half-walked, half-dragged him back and forth across the small room. On the bed, Dexter groaned in agony.

Buzzy started mumbling, "Walk into a saloon for a nice

little drink and I end up playin' nursemaid to a drunk doc and a snot-nosed twerp what ain't got the sense the Good Lord done give a jackrabbit."

"I think you've got the situation pegged, Mr. Oathammer," Fargo said.

Doc Phipps was feeling no pain, unlike most of his patients that evening. He and Edmond McNiff, the editor of the *Paradise Telegram*—and Doc's partner in insobriety—had enjoyed an evening of soused poker together in the back room of the *Telegram*'s office.

They marched Doc Phipps back and forth across the wooden floor while Dexter continued moaning on the bed. Ma Fisher came in every now and then to pump scalding coffee, laced with large quantities of salt, down Phipps's throat.

"Mind he don't upchuck his dinner all over y'all," Ma Fisher commented to Fargo and Buzzy, after feeding him the seventh cup of salty java.

No sooner did Ma make for the door then Phipps turned and erupted, spraying Fargo and Buzzy with pungent puke. He staggered away and collapsed into a chair. He pulled a filthy handkerchief from his coat pocket and wiped his forehead.

"I've been ambushed," Buzzy angrily shouted, wiping puke from his face.

"That goes double for me," Fargo said, doing the same.

"My apologies, gentlemen," Doc Phipps said, mopping his brow and tossing the soiled white rag aside. "These things happen."

10

The sun inched its way up into a slate-gray sky as Doc Phipps, more or less sober now, finished bandaging Dexter all up. Dexter's face was covered with strips of cotton; one eye was swollen shut. Phipps had wrapped tape around Dexter's midsection, which was a sea of purple splotches.

"Bless my soul," Buzzy cackled. "The boy looks like a hundred forty pounds of condemned chicken livers."

Dexter rolled in and out of awareness, uttering a lot of nonsensical babble now and then. At one point, as Doc Phipps treated his cuts with iodine, Dexter's eyes flew open and he cried, "Don't eat Mr. Klapsattle's pigeons, Harvey."

"Who's Mr. Klapsattle?" Buzzy wanted to know.

"What are pigeons?" Fargo asked in return.

"I dunno," Buzzy said, "but Harvey seems to like 'em."

Doc Phipps finished treating Dexter's wounds and said, "Looks worse than he is. A couple of bruised ribs, slight concussion, and enough lacerations to keep him out of any beauty pageants for the foreseeable future." He corked up the iodine bottle and said, "Somebody want to tell me how this happened?"

"I tried to send him home," Fargo said. "He came back."

"He got any kin?" Doc Phipps asked.

"A mother and a brother," Fargo said. "Back in New York City, where he hails from."

"He won't be going back there anytime soon," Doc Phipps said. "I don't want him moving from this bed for at least a week."

"A week?" Fargo asked. "I was hoping to put him on the six-thirty to Fort Worth." He was thinking of the Danbys; it was mostly what he thought about since his chat with Marshal Fix. And he didn't want Dexter Tritt getting caught in the middle of anything. The memory of Eddie Buzzell was still fresh in Fargo's mind.

"Out of the question," Doc Phipps said. "This boy needs time to heal proper, and he won't do it bumping around all over the territory."

He pulled a bottle of laudanum out of his bag and handed it to Fargo, saying, "Give him a few nips of this every few hours once he wakes up. He'll need it. When it's done, come see me for more."

Fargo looked at the bottle and said, "I hear tell this stuff is what you call habit-formin'."

"Yes, it is, very much so," Doc Phipps said. "But it's the least of his problems."

Ma Fisher opened the door and stuck her head inside, blurting out, "The coffee's hot and the eggs are gettin' colder than a spinster's titty. Y'all get down here to breakfast and leave that boy in peace."

Ma Fisher and her daughter Prudie served them eggs and fried potatoes and bread with real butter and strawberry jam. Fargo, Buzzy, and Doc Phipps sipped her wonderful coffee gratefully. It had been a long night, and Ma Fisher made the best coffee in Paradise.

Fargo speared a fried egg and popped it into his mouth. He watched Prudie Fisher as she stood at the stove tending to a pot of simmering oatmeal. As the sun's early morning rays shot through the kitchen window, he could see her slender, curvy form under her thin dress. She was definitely someone he wanted to get to know better, and he would have tried had Ma Fisher not kicked him in the leg as he sat chewing egg and trying to imagine what Prudie looked like naked.

"The lusts of men sicken me, Mr. Fargo," Ma said, "especially when it's my daughter they're lustin' after." At the stove, Prudie giggled.

Fargo went back to his eggs, declining comment. Buzzy snorted, trying to keep a mouthful of Ma's fried potatoes from shooting out of his nose. He cackled, "Caught y'all starin' at Prudie, didn't she?"

"You shut up, too, you old goat," Ma Fisher said, and clunked her fist on Buzzy's head.

"Damn, woman," Buzzy said, and rubbed his skull. I was just havin' fun, is all."

"Ain't no fool like an old fool," Ma Fisher said. She grabbed a serving tray from the breakfront and slapped a soup bowl on top of it. She shoved the tray at her nubile daughter and ordered, "Fill that bowl with some beef broth, Prudence, and take it up to that poor soul upstairs. Iffen he's a friend of Skye Fargo's, odds are he won't be takin' no solid food for a spell."

"Yes, Mama," Prudie said, and grabbed a ladle.

On the stove a pot of beef barley soup was simmering for Monday lunch. Prudie dipped the ladle into the soup and came out with some deep dark broth. She clumsily splashed some into the bowl, slopping it all over the floor. Carrying the tray, she made her way over to the kitchen larder and grabbed a handful of soda crackers. She dropped them onto the tray and sashayed through the swinging kitchen doors. Fargo heard her footsteps running up the staircase. Spearing a piece of greasy potato, he wondered how big her nipples were. He looked up at Ma guiltily. She was frying up more eggs, her back to him. Fargo made a note in his head to try and win her confidence. He'd need it, if Prudie was the reward.

Prudie made it up to Dexter's room with a good quarter inch of soup still in the bowl. She kicked the door open and made a beeline over to the bed, where Dexter was writhing in pain, tossing and turning and sounding miserable.

Prudie placed the tray on the night table and gently rolled Dexter onto his back. His eyes opened for a split second. Still slightly delirious, he looked up at Prudie and grinned like a half-idiot. He said, "Are we having waffles today, Mama?"

"No waffles," Prudie said, grabbing the bowl of soup and a spoon. "Just Mama's beef barley soup."

Dexter tried to sit up, and was rewarded with waves of pain cascading through every inch of his being. Even his hair hurt, if that was possible. He sank back down onto the pillow with an audible groan. "I don't feel so good," he said.

"No, I don't expect you do," Prudie said, "after what you've been through."

"Where am I, exactly?" Dexter asked, and winced. Talking hurt, too.

"You're at my ma's boarding house," Prudie said. "Mr. Fargo and Buzzy Oathammer brought you here last night."

She sat on the edge of the bed and set the tray down so that it was in close proximity to his mouth. She crumpled up some soda crackers and dropped them into the thick, tasty broth.

"Do I look as bad as I feel?" Dexter asked, although he pretty much knew the answer.

"You look like someone who was stuffed ass over teakettle into a pi-ano, if that answers your question," Prudie said.

"I guess it does," Dexter replied.

Prudie spooned some of the soup, which did smell tempting. She raised it to his mouth, saying, "Now open wide, Mr. Tritt."

Dexter did, and swallowed with some difficulty. Soup squirted from the corner of his mouth and dribbled down his left cheek. His jawed ached and his throat felt hotter than the cobblestones on Delancey Street in the middle of

August. Prudie held out another spoonful of broth. Dexter waved it away.

"Thank you, but eating hurts too much right now," he said.

"I think we can fix that," Prudie said, getting up and setting the tray down on top of the chest of drawers. She picked up the bottle of laudanum Doc Phipps left and uncorked it with her teeth. She took the spoon from the soup bowl and sat down on the edge of the bed again.

"Have some of this, Mr. Tritt," she said, pouring some of the elixir into the spoon.

"What is it?" Dexter asked.

"Medicine," Prudie responded. "Make you feel much better."

Anything that would make him feel better, Dexter was all for. He slurped the laudanum off the spoon. It tasted like gutter water, but heavier. He knew the taste of gutter water firsthand, having had his face pushed into a big black puddle of it on Knickerbocker Street when he was nine, courtesy of Otis Fleagle, the neighborhood bully.

Prudie poured another into the spoon. "Have more," she said. It slid down Dexter's gullet and into his belly, where it made him feel all nice and warm inside. Things got fuzzy in his head, but the pain wasn't nearly as it was before.

"Feeling better, Mr. Tritt?" Prudie asked.

Now that the pain was just about gone and he was floating on a cloud, Dexter looked at Prudie and decided she was the best-looking thing he'd seen since arriving in Texas. He said, "As a matter of fact, yes." He looked at her again and said, "I don't even know your name."

"It's Prudence, but everyone calls me Prudie," she said.

"Can I be an everyone, Prudie?" Dexter asked.

"In Texas, Mr. Tritt, it's proper for gentleman to address me as *Miss* Prudie," she said.

Words seemed to slide out of Dexter's mouth, as if he

had no control over them. "You're very, very Prudie, Miss Pretty."

Prudie giggled and said, "If this stuff makes you think I'm pretty, then maybe you better have more." She poured, and Dexter got the stuff down easily this time. He even licked the spoon.

"Don't you think you're pretty?" he asked.

Prudie blushed just a little and said, "Are you flirting with me, Mr. Tritt?"

Dexter hadn't really considered it, not that he was able to consider anything at the moment. The laudanum was hitting him hard. He'd never felt so good in all his born days.

"I dunno," Dexter said. "I never flirted with anyone before."

"Then you're in no condition to start now, is my guess," Prudie said. "You best get some sleep now, Mr. Tritt." She pulled the covers up to his chin and said, "Nighty night."

"Isn't it daytime?" Dexter asked.

"In a couple of minutes, you won't know the difference," she said.

"Will you come back and see me again?" Dexter asked.

"I suspect I'll have to, until you get well," she said, "and you won't get well sittin' there flapping your tongue."

The door opened, and Doc Phipps and Fargo walked in. Doc Phipps asked Prudie, "So how's our young patient?"

"I'm flying on a cloud of love," Dexter said, his eyeballs rolling in their sockets.

Doc Phipps picked up the laudanum bottle and turned to Prudie, "Good Lord, little lady—how much of this stuff did you give him?"

"Was it too much?"

"Any amount of laudanum is too much," Doc Phipps said. "Especially to a tinhorn like this Easterner."

"He gonna be all right?" Fargo asked.

"He'll be right as rain in about ten hours," Doc Phipps said. "In the meantime, I reckon he's floatin' somewhere over St. Louis. Might have to strap his dumb city ass down before he makes it over the Atlantic."

For no discernible reason at all, Dexter cried out, "I hate Otis Fleagle!"

Fargo turned to Doc Phipps and asked, "Who the hell is Otis Fleagle?"

Dexter's eyes were glazed over like a cold fog rolling in off the Hudson River. A dreamy, dopey grin was plastered across his face and, as an added touch, he was drooling all over the blanket.

"Was I you, Fargo, I wouldn't wait for an answer," Doc Phipps said. "Not if you got any plans for the day."

11

They came at daybreak, eight in all. They brought their mounts to a halt at the top of a ridge half a mile from the town of Mineral Springs, a three-day ride from Paradise.

An achingly cold wind blew down from the Oklahoma Territories. A couple of the men shivered. Hoke Danby did not. Instead, he stared down at Mineral Springs, working a wad of tobacco back up into his cheek. He spit a huge blast of brown juice off to the side. Mineral Springs, a rathole of a Texas town. He spit again, a testament to those who planned to hang his brother Earl at high noon that very day. Even now, the good people of Mineral Springs were busy as beavers, erecting the gallows that would, in a few short hours, be used to stretch Earl's neck like warm taffy.

Earl had journeyed to Texas, accompanied by his brothers Jimmy and Luke, to scout out some future business prospects. The ignorant peckerhead got two of the Danby's killed, shooting up Mineral Springs in the process, and now the townsfolk wanted blood. Hoke was tempted to let Earl hang, but in the end there was no question about his mission—Danby blood was not shed lightly; anybody who killed a Danby was a marked man forever.

The West Arkansas hills were home to over a hundred Danbys, not to mention a huge passel of their equally mean-spirited cousins, the Gorch and Gribble clans.

He wiped his mouth on the back of his sleeve. He was a tall man from a family of smaller men, almost six foot, big for a Danby. He was lean, with a thin face and penetrating coal-black eyes that bespoke the darkest sins of man.

To his left, Chigger Danby, Hoke's nineteen-year-old half brother, asked, "You reckon this is such a good idea, Hoke?"

"Might be they's settin' to ambush us," said Ferd Danby, another Danby brother, meaner than a rattlesnake at the tender age of fifteen.

Hoke said nothing, staring grimly down at Mineral Springs. Instead, a voice piped up on Hoke's right, saying, "Shut yer yaps, all y'all. Hoke knows what he's doin'."

Hoke glanced over at the talker, his baby sister, Violet, just turned seventeen—and what a seventeen. Nice firm jugs that tried to burst out of her skintight red shirt; a full, fluffy head of blond hair, not the stiff, strawlike red that was a Danby trademark. Where Violet came by her astonishingly good looks was a matter of much conjecture amongst the Danby clan. Rumor had it that Violet's daddy was a traveling salesman who got a little too frisky with their mama one muggy August night eighteen years ago whilst their pappy, Lemuel, was off hunting up in the hills.

It was all Hoke could do to keep his cousins' and even his brothers' filthy paws off her. Not that Violet needed any help; she could fire a pistol or fling a blade farther than all of her brothers—except Hoke. He was ten years her senior and was the only other Danby she truly feared and respected. And sort of loved in a way she knew wasn't entirely healthy. Sometimes her nipples got all hard and tingly when he looked at her that certain way, like he was now.

Hoke gave his little sister host of a ghost of a smile. "We stick to the plan," he said. "Anyone don't like it, I'll cut 'em from neck to nuts." He dismounted and walked to the edge of the ridge. The gallows was all but finished. Time was short.

Nathan and Packy Gribble, nineteen and twenty respectively, wisely kept their mouths shut. As the Arkansas Gribbles went, Nathan and Packy were among the vilest, meanest, and most merciless that the clan had to offer, but they knew their place.

Lyle Gorch, Jeeter's sixteen-year-old brother, had not been blessed with such wisdom. "You shore Earl's down there, Hoke? If he ain't, we come all this way for nothin' and yer plan ain't fer shit."

Stupid peckerhead, Jeeter thought, and that was all it took. Hoke was on Lyle in half a second, yanking him off his horse. Lyle went flying and hit the ground with a thud that could be heard in the next county, knocking the wind out of him. Before he could catch his breath, Hoke kicked him solidly in the ribs, sending Lyle rolling onto his back.

The sidewinder was quick. Gasping for air, Lyle cleared leather and aimed straight for Hoke's head. There was a pretty good chance Lyle would have succeeded in killing him had Violet not been quicker. She drew her pistol and squeezed off one shot—which was enough. The bullet slammed into Lyle's wrist. His gun jumped from his grip and skittered off. Lyle caught his breath long enough to start howling in agony, his hand looking like a bloody slab of beef.

Hoke pulled the whip from his back pocket. It was his pride and joy, made from the finest aged leather. He'd studded it with two dozen filed-down two-penny nails for extra fun. He cracked the whip a couple of times to get his rhythm, then brought the full force of his fury down on his cousin, giving him a solid lash across the face.

Lyle wailed in pain. "Do 'im good, Hoke," Violet said breathlessly.

Hoke thrashed him mercilessly across the face and chest. Lyle uselessly tried to dodge the lashings, holding his arms in front of his face until his arms were covered with bloody gashes.

Violet was all atwitter, egging her brother on. "Hurt him,

big brother. Make him bleed." Damn if her nipples weren't getting hard again.

Lyle curled up into a little ball and tried to roll away. Hoke gave him what-for, going to work on Lyle's back. The studded whip ripped through the thin fabric of his shirt until his back was crisscrossed with red slits. Jeeter made no move to help his baby brother. Served the little shitbox right for mouthing off, a sentiment the rest of the gang felt, more or less.

Not even breaking a sweat, Hoke gave Lyle a few more lashes for luck, his anger finally spent. Lyle was whimpering meekly, the tears stinging the wounds on his face. For Violet, it wasn't quite enough. She hopped off her horse and strode over to Hoke. She grabbed the whip from his hand and raised it up, ready to deliver one last agonizing strike. Hoke laughed and snatched the whip away from her.

"Don't kill him, for corn's sake. He's still kin, even if he ain't no smarter'n a turkey buzzard."

Violet turned to Hoke indignantly. "You never let me have no fun."

Hoke ignored her. He kicked Lyle a couple of times, saying, "Git up, you stinkin' lousy puke, or do you want more?" When Lyle didn't move, Hoke turned to Jeeter and said, "Git him on his horse. They's work to do." He added, "And while you're at it, teach him some manners."

Jeeter silently climbed off his horse and went to tend to his brother, who was still whimpering and wiping blood and snot from his nose. Hoke grabbed Violet's ass, a shade more firmly than the situation demanded, and pushed her toward her horse. "You mount up too, girl."

Violet felt her womanly part get all warm and moist. She'd rub it against the saddlehorn, as she often did when she rode with Hoke, but it was never quite enough.

"Everyone know what-all they's supposed to do when we get there?" Hoke asked, and was greeted by nods all around.

"Fine," Hoke said. "Now let's go git my brother Earl. Or do any of you gophers got a better idea?"

None of the gophers did.

"I ain't eatin' this pig slop," Earl Danby cried, flinging the plate of beans and grits at the bars of his cell. The ten-cent blue plate special from the café shattered against the steel bars and sent breakfast splattering all over Marshal Horace Pinkley's uniform as well as his face.

Pinkley wiped buttered grits from his eyes and said to Earl, "If you wasn't scheduled to hang at high noon, I'd blast you into the middle of next week."

"And if you wasn't uglier than a pimple on a bullfrog's butt," Earl shot back, grinning, "I'd ask you to marry me."

Pinkley grabbed a rag from a nearby bucket and wiped the mess off his face, saying, "Smile now, pond scum. You won't be smilin' in a coupla hours when we slip that rope around your worthless gullet."

Earl laughed heartily, though there was no mirth in it. He said, "You best let me go. Ain't nobody hangs a Danby and lives to tell about it."

"Even if that *was* true, which it ain't," Pinkley declared, "It'd still be worth it to watch your rotten carcass swing in the breeze."

The door to the jailhouse creaked open, and in came another pain in the ass. Reverend Eustace Meeks, looking slightly holier-than-thou, strolled in, clutching his beloved Bible. He was a man who tried to see the good in all, and firmly opposed the shedding of blood in the name of law and order. He was a balding, fussy-looking man, no more than five feet-two inches tall, with wire-frame spectacles that seemed to dwarf his shiny face. He clutched the Good Book to his breast, prepared to provide comfort and spiritual guidance to the condemned man, a grim task—and, the saints be praised, Earl Danby was laughing.

89

Reverend Meeks said to Pinkley, "Well, I see our young friend hasn't lost his sense of humor."

"Sense of humor," Pinkley snorted. "Ain't nothin' funny about getting yourself hung. You ask me, he's a coupla pickles short of a barrel." To Meeks, he said testily, "What do you want, Reverend?"

"It's time for Earl to make his peace with the Almighty, Horace," Reverend Meeks said.

"There ain't that much time if you and me live two hundred years, Reverend," Pinkley said, wiping the last of the greasy beans off his vest. "Can't this wait?"

Reverend Meeks shook his head and said solemnly, "It's never too soon to take Jesus into your heart."

"I ain't so sure Earl's got one, Reverend," Pinkley said. "But give it your best shot."

"Thank you, Marshal," Meeks said, and grabbed a chair. He sat down next to the cell, facing the condemned man. "And how are we today, Earl?"

Earl looked at him quizzically and said, "We? You seein' double, holy man?"

Meeks said, "I meant the collective 'we,' Earl."

"The what?" Earl asked.

Reverend Meeks wisely decided against pursuing this avenue of discussion and pressed on, asking Earl, "Are you ready to accept Jesus Christ as your one and only Lord and savior?"

"The only words of your'n I know is Jesus and Christ and Lord, and they don't mean jack-shit to me." With that, he hawked a particularly large and slimy brown goober up his throat and spit it square through the bars and onto Reverend Meeks's black tie. "Go screw a goat," Earl said.

Meeks looked down at his soiled tie with grim distaste. Sitting at his desk, legs up, Horace Pinkley laughed harshly. "You ain't a-gonna bring him over to your side, Preacher, no matter what," he chuckled.

Reverend Meeks ignored the marshal and attempted to

press on in the manner as befitted a servant of the Almighty, not to mention holding onto his last shred of dignity. "That wasn't very Christian, Earl," he said.

Horace Pinkley shook his head in disgust. He had little use for Reverend Meeks, or for preachermen in general. To his way of thinking, they were good only for women and children and the weak of heart. Wasn't no religion better than two loaded barrels and some hot lead into the belly of anyone who didn't respect the laws of the land.

He continued, "That dog fart ain't got a Christian bone in his body, Reverend. Lookit what he and his brothers did, all that killin' and rapin' and thievin'. The sooner that boy's dancin' on the end of a rope, the sounder we'll all sleep at night."

"We're all children of the Lord," Reverend Meeks said, with some heat. "Maybe the worst of us even more so."

"Yeah, well, whatever," Pinkley said, rising from the desk. It was time to see to hammering the last nail into the gallows and then head on over to the hotel, where the hangman, Jonah Quimby, was sleeping off an all-night bender. Quimby had been imported all the way from San Angelo at the exorbitant fee of two hundred dollars, a pretty fair chunk of change for a small town like Mineral Springs. Pinkley had been content to string Earl Danby up to the nearest live oak and be done with it. Seeing how Earl and his brothers had killed three people in their attempt to rob the bank, however, the town council, headed by Mayor Mortimer Paroo, were out for blood. There was nothing like a public hanging to demonstrate to any outlaw in the territory that Mineral Springs was anything but easy pickings.

Pinkley grabbed the tools of his trade—a rifle and a six-shooter—and plucked his hat off a nail by the door. He said to Meeks, "Make it quick, Preacher. Soon as I can get Quimby sobered up, Earl's got a date with him."

Reverend Meeks grimaced and wiped the slime from his

necktie. Gallows. Hangmen. Public executions. It was downright un-Christian. Death and dying were the Lord's business, not man's.

He opened his Bible and said to Earl, "Are you ready to repent for your sins and find true salvation, Earl? I'm here to help you."

"You wanna help me," Earl said. "You can let me go afore that lawman comes back."

"You know I can't do that, son," Reverend Meeks said. "Why the very idea! Marshal Pinkley would have my head on a silver platter."

"Then I got no use fer y'all," Earl said. "Git the hell out of my face you son of a whore."

Reverend Meeks blanched, but tried to keep his composure. "Earl—"

"Your momma was nothing but a *cheap whore*!" Earl bellowed, gripping the thick steel bars of the jail cell and shaking them like a man possessed. His face was beet-red; spittle dotted his thin lips. At that moment, he reminded Meeks of a rabid mongrel.

"Repent now, boy!" Reverend Meeks cried, jumping up from his chair. Two could play at this game. "Repent or be damned to the scorching flames of eternal hellfire!"

"Whore!" Earl's left hand shot out through the bars like a bolt of lightening and grabbed a fistful of Meeks's stiffly starched shirt. He yanked Meeks toward him and the reverend's face slammed into the bars, smashing his nose and stunning him. Both of Earl's hands lashed out and curled tightly around the Reverend Meeks's gullet with the single-minded intention of crushing his windpipe.

He likely would have succeeded had Marshal Pinkley not returned to fetch some invoices off his desk that needed Mayor Paroo's signature. Reverend Meeks was turning a bright shade of purple, eyeballs protruding hideously from their sockets. Pinkley dashed over to the cell and grabbed Meeks by the collar, yanking him away with a fair amount of effort. He was half tempted to let Earl finish the job and be shut of the pesky, self-righteous preacher, but what was the point? The town would just go out and find themselves another.

"Next time you won't be so lucky!" Earl shouted.

"You shut the hell up, Earl," Pinkley said, "or I'll shoot you now."

He led Reverend Meeks over to his chair and sat him down. Blood streamed from Meeks's crushed nose and splattered all over his shirt. The reverend pulled a hanky from his inside jacket pocket and placed it over his nose to staunch the bleeding.

"Put your head back, Reverend," Pinkley said. He went and fetched another rag and handed it to Meeks. "Try this."

"Thank you kindly," Meeks said, his voice muffled.

"Tried to warn you, Reverend," Pinkley said. "Some souls just can't be saved. You best get yourself over to Doc Dubbins and have that snout of yours looked at. Could be broke."

Reverend Meeks mumbled something from under the rag, but Pinkley never heard it. An ear-shattering, teeth-rattling roar ripped through the warm late morning air. A window in the front jailhouse wall blew in, spraying glass everywhere. Reverend Meeks tumbled out of the chair and banged his noggin on the wooden floor, knocking him senseless. Pinkley flung himself into a corner to avoid the shattering glass. In that split second before the explosion subsided, Pinkley knew at once what had caused it: dynamite.

It wasn't much, really.

Nathan and Packy Gribble had trotted as easy as you please into Mineral Springs, two trail-dusty saddletramps who might have been headed to the Bull's Breath Saloon to wet their whistles with some warm beer. They rode in un-noticed by the townsfolk, who were still on their guard from the last raid on their town. Today, though, was sort of like a holiday. Earl Danby was being hung, and there would be barbecue and cotton candy and strong apple cider for one and all. The people were just gearing up for the festivities and the excitement was running high.

Nathan and Packy Gribble cantered a few hundred yards down the main street of Mineral Springs and stopped in front of Appleyard's Mercantile. They both reached into their saddlebags and pulled out a stick of dynamite each. Nathan struck a match on the side of his blue jeans and lit the fuse on his stick, then lit the fuse on Packy's stick. The fuses sparkled brightly as the Gribble brothers giggled and tossed the dynamite sticks through the open door of the Appleyard Mercantile, then put spurs to flanks and galloped hell for leather down Main Street.

The dynamite landed a few inches from a keg of two-penny nails. The mercantile erupted into flames. Moments later, farther down and across the street, Lyle and Jeeter Gorch tossed two sticks of dynamite toward the batwing doors of the Pickled Okra saloon, where they fell a foot or so shy of the entrance. Lyle and Jeeter beat a hasty retreat. Inside, more than a dozen of the menfolk were having a prehanging celebration. It might have been a convenient quirk of fate, or perhaps the will of the Almighty, but at the exact moment the dynamite hit the wooden-plank sidewalk, bartender Chester Shottish was heaving the contents of the spittoon out into the street. As the mercantile exploded, Shottish was knocked onto his side, the contents of the spittoon spilling all over the sizzling dynamite fuses, extinguishing them.

The scene on Main Street was chaos. Women screamed and children bawled, as the men scrambled to their feet and went running toward Appleyard's Mercantile. In the confusion, nobody noticed Chigger and Ferd Danby stroll nonchalantly into the Mineral Springs Bank.

Meanwhile, inside the jailhouse, Horace Pinkley rose

shakily to his feet. Luther Heggs, who owned the barber-shop next door to the jail, burst through the door and cried out, "It's the mercantile, Horace! It's done blowed up and burnin' like a tinderbox!"

Either Amos Appleyard had gotten careless with the TNT again—it wouldn't be the first time—or something much worse was happening. Pinkley took no chances. He rummaged through his desk and pulled out a box of cartridges. He started loading his Colt and said to Luther Heggs, "Well, don't just stand there like a fencepost. Get the bucket brigade going before half the town goes up in flames."

Luther Heggs nodded and took off. Four shots rang out, and a second later the pudgy little barber staggered backward through the open jailhouse door, clutching his belly. Pinkley dropped his Colt as Luther fell into Pinkley's arms, blood spurting from the holes in his gut.

Luther Heggs tried to speak; his lips moved, but no sounds came out. He died with his eyes wide open and slid from Pinkley's grasp onto the floor. Two figures appeared in the doorway, a hard-eyed, scruffy-looking dude and a girl, their guns drawn and aimed at Pinkley. He'd never seen them before, but knew instinctively who they were. There was no time to go for his gun. They had him, dead to center.

From the cell, Pinkley heard Earl Danby say, "It's about time you chunkheads got here. Another hour an' I woulda been dead."

Hoke Danby looked at the tin star pinned to Horace Pinkley's vest with a special brand of cold hatred reserved solely for lawmen. Never taking his eyes off Pinkley, he said to Earl, "You don't shut your stupid craw, boy, I'll kill you my ownself."

Hoke cocked his pistol and said to Pinkley, "Now what's all this horseshit 'bout hangin' my baby brother?"

* * *

Alexander Botts was down on his hands and knees, picking up the coins. He'd been carrying the tray from the safe to the teller's cage when the explosion shook the whole building, knocking Alexander flat on his bony ass. His father, Wellington Botts, owner of the Mineral Springs Bank, had gone over to the café to have his noon dinner, leaving Alexander to run the place all by his lonesome. They needed to hire a new teller or two, but nobody wanted the job, not after Earl Danby and his brothers had slaughtered the last two in their botched robbery attempt.

Slightly dazed from the explosion, Alexander groped around the floor for the coins, some of which had rolled into a rathole. The sound of the eruption had emanated from the vicinity of Appleyard's Mercantile.

Alexander was reaching for some pennies when he sensed, rather than saw, shadows fall over him. Probably his father back from the café and ready to scream at him again for something—it didn't matter what. His father seemingly enjoyed screaming and berating him for transgressions real or imagined. Now nineteen, Alexander had had enough. He'd managed to squirrel away almost two hundred dollars by filching a dollar here and there, usually right under his father's nose. When his ill-gotten grubstake had reached two hundred fifty dollars, Alexander planned to spit squarely in his father's fat face and take the next stage to either Fort Worth or Houston, hopefully never to return.

Alexander looked up and saw two men standing over him, pointing pistols at his head.

Alexander stared at them dumbly. They weren't men at all, but boys, sixteen or seventeen at the most, and from the looks of them, hadn't seen anything close to soap and water for ages.

Chigger said to Alexander, "Stand and deliver!" He'd heard Hoke say that once, back when they'd robbed that stagecoach over in Bentonville.

"Stand and what?" Alexander asked, still on his hands and knees.

"It means this here's a robbery," Ferd informed him.

"You're robbing the bank?" Alexander asked. This couldn't be happening, not again, not so soon after the last time.

Chigger pressed the barrel of his pistol flat onto Alexander's nose and cocked the trigger. He said, "What the hell you think 'stand and deliver' means, you ignorant peckerhead? Now open the safe."

Alexander rose nervously to his feet. "I ain't got the combination—my daddy has it, and he ain't here," he stammered.

Chigger eyed him coolly, then said, "I think you're lying, mister." He fired a shot into Alexander's left leg. Alexander howled in pain and crashed to the floor.

Chigger said, "I'll ask you agin. What's the combination?"

"I don't know!" Alexander wailed. "Daddy don't trust me with the big money!"

Alexander whimpered, clutching his wounded leg. Just then, a chubby, balding man, a napkin still tucked under his three chins, came running in, his face sweaty and flushed with excitement.

"Lock the doors, Alexander," the chubby man was yammering. "Take all the money—" He saw Alexander writhing in pain on the floor, his leg a bloody mess, and said, "What in the name of Christ—"

"You must be Daddy," Ferd said.

Wellington Botts asked angrily, "What the devil have you done to my boy?"

"He wouldn't tell us the combination to the safe," Chigger said. "Claims you don't trust him."

"It's a sad day when a daddy don't trust his own kin," Ferd said.

Wellington Botts screamed, "Get the hell out of my bank, you prairie rats! You'll get nothing from me."

"Have it your own way, fatty," Chigger said, and shot Alexander in the other leg, an inch below the kneecap. Alexander flopped around like a trout out of water and cried out in agony.

"For Chrissakes, open it, Pa!" he begged, blood streaming from his wounded legs.

"You shut up, you coward!" Wellington Botts said.

"The next one goes in his sweetmeats," Chigger said. "Lessen you open that safe."

Botts was sweating like a stuck pig. He wiped his fleshy brow with the napkin and said, "The safe is empty, I swear it. It's never—"

Chigger aimed and fired another shot into Alexander, hitting him in the left shoulder, not in the sweetmeats, as he'd threatened. No reason to make the son suffer any more than he had to just because his father was a fool. Alexander cried out again.

"You gonna open it now?" Chigger asked. "Or do I have to kill him?"

Wellington Botts hurried over to the safe and spun the dial to the left, then to the right, and then back to the left again. He yanked it open, reached in, and started tossing stacks of paper money at the Danbys, muttering, "Twice in one month. This is the last time I open a bank in this godforsaken territory . . ."

Chigger and Ferd scooped up the money and stuffed it into a small burlap sack. Chigger said to the fat banker, "You coulda saved your boy a whole lotta hurtin' iffen you'd been smarter, mister."

"Yeah," Ferd agreed. "You ain't very nice, fatty."

"You can go straight to hell, you scum!" Botts said by way of reply.

Chigger pumped two shots into Wellington Botts. One

took him an inch above the left eye; the other in the neck. Botts dropped to the floor like a sack of brass doorknobs.

Ferd examined the two bullet holes in Wellington Botts and commented, "Pretty sloppy shootin' there, Chigger."

"Yeah? Ya think?" Chigger responded. He whirled around and squeezed off the last round in the chamber, straight into Alexander Botts's heart. Alexander flopped again, then lay still.

"That was better," Ferd said as they strolled out of the bank.

Reverend Meeks cowered in terror as he watched Hoke Danby put two bullets into Horace Pinkley's heart. Pinkley was dead before he hit the floor.

Violet had taken the keys and released Earl from the cell. Earl spit on Pinkley's lifeless body, and said, "I'll see you in hell, lawman."

"You are the toughest talkin' blowhard I ever seen," Hoke said to Earl impatiently, pushing Earl toward the door.

"What about him, Hoke?" Violet asked, pointing to Reverend Meeks, who was shaking uncontrollably in the corner, clutching his Bible.

"Go on out and mount up, both of you," Hoke said. "I'll handle him."

When they were gone, Hoke said to Reverend Meeks, "I hope Earl weren't too much trouble."

"None at all," Reverend Meeks said, his voice unsteady.

"Earl's a good boy, mostly," Hoke said, " 'cept he ain't got one itty bitty brain in his whole head."

He shot Reverend Meeks twice, then holstered his pistol. He said, "Takes all kinds to make a world."

An hour after the Danby gang rode out of Mineral Springs, half the town was in flames. And for all their efforts, it was unlikely that the townsfolk would be able to save the other half.

At dusk, they made camp by a creek ridged on either side by a copse of tall cottonwoods. Violet set to preparing the evening meal—beans and bacon and biscuits that were slightly less hard than the rocks in the West Texas soil. None of the gang dared complain about Violet's appalling lack of culinary skills, however. Packy Gribble had once made the mistake of saying Violet's beans looked and tasted like rabbit turds. Violet whacked him over the noggin with a cast-iron skillet, knocking him flat on his ass. Packy saw double for a week.

The gang was tired but exhilarated as well—nothing got their juices flowing better than wreaking death and destruction on an unsuspecting populace. They set about cooling down their horses, starting a campfire, and getting settled in for the evening. Bottles of rotgut were passed around. The mood was festive.

While the others were celebrating, Hoke counted the purloined bank money. Almost five hundred dollars—not bad for a little shithole bank in a little shithole town. He stuffed the cash back into the sack and stuffed it into his saddlebags, to be distributed to the gang whenever the hell he felt like doling it out. There would be no complaints from the others.

He walked over to the campfire, where Violet was stirring beans and the others were sucking down hooch. Earl was saying, halfway to drunkenness, ". . . Ain't no way they woulda hung me, not in a month of Sundays. Why, I coulda busted out of that ol' jail anytime I was of a mind to."

"That ain't what it looked like to us," Lyle Gorch said.

"Yeah," Nathan Gribble added. "I bet even money you'da shit your britches when they put that rope around your gullet."

"I'll shit in your hat, you ignorant toad," Earl said in reply.

"Like that time up in Jonesboro," Jeeter Gorch said.

"When we took that stagecoach an' the shotgun got off two shots before we blasted him. Y'all recollect when Earl went piddly in his pants he was so scairt?"

They all had a good laugh over that memory. Earl's ears got hot and he got all wrathy. To his left, Chigger was downing the last of the brown bottle of hooch. Earl grabbed the pistol from Chigger's holster and would have pumped a couple of shots into the nearest tormentor had Hoke not kicked the gun out of his hand, sending it skittering into the dirt a few feet away. The laughter died quickly.

"You best learn to control yer temper, boy," Hoke said.

"But Hoke," Earl pleaded. "They's sayin' I pissed my pants when that weren't what happened a-tall—"

"Lets you an' me have us a little confab, little brother," Hoke said, and gestured for Earl to follow him. Hoke walked off, away from the campfire. Earl scurried off behind him as the others went back to their drinking. There were more titters; Earl knew they were laughing at him, and his ears burned some more.

Regardless, he chattered away as he followed Hoke, saying, "How much we get from the bank, Hoke? When you gonna divvy it, Hoke? A pretty penny, I bet. Who we a-gonna hit next, Hoke? I can't wait—"

When they were deeper into the wooded area, Hoke stopped abruptly, turned to Earl, and rammed his fist hard into Earl's belly, knocking the wind out of him.

Earl fell to his knees, clutching his midsection and gasped for air. He croaked, "What-all you do that fer, Hoke?"

Hoke said nothing. He grabbed a big clump of Earl's thin, greasy hair and jerked his brother to his feet. Earl cried out in pain. Hoke hauled off and slapped the left side of Earl's baby face, then backhanded him on the right side. Earl's head whipped back and forth from the force of the blows. He made no effort to fight back; doing so would mean certain death.

"You backwoods no-neck pisspot," Hoke said, slapping his brother silly. "Ignorant little chunkhead." He pushed Earl away. Earl landed with a thump on his ass and started crying. Hoke said, "I shoulda let 'em hang your worthless hide."

"What'd I do?" Earl asked, trying not to cry. "I ain't done nothin'."

"Two of your brothers is dead," Hoke said, resisting the urge to wallop Earl into mincemeat. "You call that nothin'?"

"I didn't kill 'em," Earl protested.

"Who did?" Hoke asked. "I wanna know."

"It were that bounty hunter out of Paradise," Earl told him. "Got the drop on us. Made no more noise'n a fart in a tailwind. He—"

"What's his name?"

"Who?" Earl asked.

"The bounty hunter, you dumb fuck!" Hoke bellowed, and made to hit Earl again.

Earl shrank away in terror. When he was certain Hoke wasn't going to thrash him again, he wiped his nose on his sleeve and tried to remember. He said, finally, "They called him Fargo. Skye Fargo, yeah, that was it. The best tracker in the whole territory is what the folks said. Put a knife right in my privates. My balls were swole somethin' awful for days."

"Is he still in Paradise?" Hoke asked.

"Dunno," Earl said. "Could be. I heared the marshal say there were a whore in town he was sorta sweet on."

"How far is this Paradise?" Hoke wanted to know.

"Couple of days' ride," Earl said. "Two, maybe three. I swear to God, Hoke—I ever see him agin, I'm a-gonna cut 'im a new butt hole."

"Oh, you'll see him agin," Hoke said. "We're all a-gonna see him. And real, real soon."

12

Fargo wanted a drink. He wanted a bunch of drinks. He had a lot on his mind.

He made his way over to Sneed Hearn's saloon and bought himself a nice bottle of whiskey. The place was empty at that time of the morning. He sat down at a table and poured himself a healthy dollop. He drank and brooded.

Marshal Fix was right—the Danbys would come. It might be a day, or a week, or even a year, but sooner or later—sooner, probably—there would be hell to pay, and the town of Paradise sat squarely in the eye of the storm.

Fargo poured himself another and tried to convince himself that leaving was the best option. Slap Dexter Tritt into a buckboard wagon, wounds and all, and hightail it to Houston or New Orleans. Send Dexter home and then . . .

Then what? Keep running? Not likely.

Fargo was lost in thought when he heard a voice ask politely, "Mind if I sit?"

He looked up—it was the stranger who'd saved his bacon the other night, the man who'd dispatched Alvin Crimp.

"Sit if you're a mind to," Fargo said to him.

The stranger sat. Fargo offered him a drink. When the stranger nodded, Fargo called to Sneed Hearn, "A glass for the stranger, Mr. Hearn. And make it a clean one, please."

Sneed Hearn brought a glass—a clean one. Fargo poured the stranger a drink. They clinked glasses.

"Cheers," Fargo said.

"*L'chaim,*" the stranger said. "In my language, that means 'to life.' "

"Works for me," Fargo said.

"So," the stranger asked, "how's your young friend? Not getting stuffed into any more pianos I hope."

"He ain't too pretty," Fargo said, "but he'll live."

"That's a goodness," the stranger said.

As Fargo poured them another, he said, "I never did get a chance to thank you proper for helping me out last night."

The stranger shrugged and said, "So say it now."

"Thanks," Fargo said. "Don't know why you done it, but thanks all the same."

"I told you why," the stranger said. "It was God's will, Mr. Fargo."

Fargo said, "You seem to know my name, but I don't know yours."

The stranger said, "I am Avram Benjamin Katz. My friends call me Nashville, like in Nashville, Tennessee. It is where my mother and I settled when we came over from the Old Country."

Nashville Katz. The name had a familiar ring. "You wouldn't be the same Nashville Katz who gunned down Pee Wee Parker up to Missouri a few years back, would you?" Fargo asked.

Katz said, "Unless there's more than one Nashville Katz running around this great country, the answer is yes." He took a sip of whiskey and added, "A most unpleasant man, that Mr. Parker. His best friends hated him."

"Unpleasant?" Fargo asked. "Pee Wee Parker was a savage."

Fargo was duly impressed. Pee Wee Parker was the worst kind of outlaw—cunning, merciless, and a back-shooter to boot. Few men took him on and lived to tell about it. He asked, "What brings you to Paradise, Mr. Katz?"

"God," Nashville Katz replied in a dry voice.

He took another swig of whiskey and grimaced. "I don't know what you paid for this *schnapps,* Mr. Fargo, but you got cheated. Oy, what I wouldn't do for some nice *slivovitz*—Jewish whiskey to you, sir."

"I'm not sure I follow you, Mr. Katz," Fargo said. "God brought you to Paradise?"

"No," Katz replied. "*I* brought *me* to Paradise. It was God's will that I make the journey."

"May I ask why?"

"You may, Mr. Fargo," Katz said. "I came to help you."

"Help me?" Fargo asked, totally flummoxed. "Help me against what?"

"Why, against the Danbys, what else?" the odd-looking stranger said. "And if you're smart, you'll give a listen to Nashville Katz."

"I'm listening," Fargo said.

"No, not here," Katz said. "Come—we'll get a little something to eat. At the café across the street. We'll eat, we'll talk. It will be a niceness."

Fargo grabbed his hat and together they left Snead Hearn's saloon and made their way over to the café. As they approached, Nashville Katz said to Fargo, "In my faith, Mr. Fargo, we have certain dietary laws. So tell me, in this establishment, you maybe know how they kill their chickens?"

"Beats me," Fargo said. "I reckon they just tell 'em flat out they're gonna die."

Katz sighed heavily and said, "Ask a stupid question . . ."

13

Gunther Toody burst through the swinging kitchen doors carrying a tray with two water glasses and a basket of freshly baked bread, then off-loaded them onto the table. His wife, Lucille, was handling the cooking today. Nashville Katz turned to Fargo, "I've been having my meals over in the hotel dining room. You can maybe recommend something nice?"

"The chili is pretty tasty," Fargo said. "Just make sure you're near a privvy in about an hour. The pork chops ain't bad, if that's your pleasure."

"From pork my people don't eat," Katz said.

"Never?" Fargo asked.

"It's a long story," Katz said. "For another time."

Playing it safe, Fargo ordered himself beefsteak with all the trimmings, and apple cobbler for dessert.

Nashville Katz opted for the fowl, asking, "How do you serve the chicken in this establishment?"

Toody looked at him quizzically. Folks in Paradise never asked that question. "On a plate," he said.

"Ask a stupid question . . ." Fargo murmured.

"I run into this problem everywhere," Katz said, and asked Toody, "Is your chicken fried in grease, in which case I don't want that. Fry a chicken, it never sits right in my belly. It clogs me up like you shouldn't know, then I'm grouchy all day long and who needs all that unpleasantness? What I want, sir, is for my chicken to be boiled for exactly six minutes."

"Six minutes?" Toody asked.

"Seven minutes is too long, five minutes is too little," Katz said. "And when it's done, you'll kindly peel off the skin."

"I will?" Toody asked.

Katz nodded and said, "Chicken skin is not a goodness. It sticks in your throat. You want I should maybe choke to death? I don't need that and neither do you. Do I speak the truth?"

Gunther Toody had been in the eats business for fifteen years all over West Texas, and knew, as all successful restaurateurs did, to cater to the whims of his diners. He nodded vigorously. "Peel the skin or the chicken gets unpleasant."

"Exactly," Katz said. "Now, with the boiled chicken— you have a vegetable that maybe was at one time the color green?"

Toody scratched his head, his brow furrowed. Before he could respond, Katz said, "If you have to think about it, then you don't."

"I have mustard pickles," Toody said. "They *used* to be green."

"He means fresh vegetables, Gunther," Fargo said, coming to Toody's rescue. "Snap beans, okra."

"No okra, thank you very much," Katz said. "It gives me, you should pardon the expression, very bad wind."

"Are you sure you don't want any okra, mister?" Toody asked.

Katz responded, "Why would I want the okra if I already said I *didn't* want the okra?"

"Because we don't have any snap beans," Toody said.

Katz wearily waved Toody away, saying, "Go and bring food for Mr. Fargo and food for me. When I get sick, I'll know who to blame."

Toddy started off for the kitchen. Fargo said, "And bring the coffee now, if you would, Gunther."

"No coffee for me," Katz said. "Instead, I'll have a nice glass of tea."

Toody looked at him incredulously, "A nice what?"

Katz opened his mouth to reply, but then thought better of it, saying, "Water is fine, thank you very much."

Toody commented, "You sure do talk funny, mister."

"You should try listening from my end," Katz said.

When Toody was gone, Katz asked Fargo, "You want it all now or after we eat?"

"What?" Fargo asked. "What brought you to Paradise?"

"You were expecting maybe a bedtime story?"

"I'm listening," Fargo said.

"It's a start," Katz said. He picked up his knife and started cleaning it on his napkin. He said, "I come from a land on the other side of the ocean. A land called Lithuania. A very pretty place, or so my mother used to tell me. Lots of trees and rivers and mountains. Unfortunately, for my people, the people of my faith, it was not such a nice place to live. The people who were not of our faith, they could come to our *shtetl*—that's a village—in the middle of the night, sometimes drunk on whiskey, sometimes not. They would burn our homes, rape our women, do whatever they wanted with no fear of the law. If we tried to fight back, it only made things worse. Then, one night when I was six years old, they came and dragged my father out of our little house. My mother and I watched as they beat him to death with big sticks and rocks. And they laughed as they killed him, Mr. Fargo. They *laughed*. It was a sound that will live with me until my dying day.

"It was always our dream to leave Lithuania and come to America, where, we were told, there was no hatred for anyone. It sounded very nice, this America. My mother, may she rest in peace, sold everything we had and very soon we were on a large boat destined for New York and a better life.

"We did not stay in New York for long. Yes, we were

free, and there were many others of our faith living there. But life was very, very harsh. People lived on top of each other, work was not easy to find, and there was more disease than hairs on your head.

"So we began on another journey, to the South this time. When I asked my mother where we were going, she said, 'We will know when we find it.' Maybe it was God's plan, or maybe we just ran out of money, but where our journey ended was in a place called Tennessee, in a town they called Nashville.

"It was a beautiful land, this Tennessee, much like the old country. My mother found work with a very nice farm family, Josephus and Arabella Nutbush and their children, Ezra and Rachel, who were close in age to me. They were Quakers, and finer people I have yet to meet in America.

"We lived on their farm and life was good. There was no more hunger and we had a roof over our heads. Then, in the summer of my fourteenth year, sickness came to the land. Typhoid, Josephus called it. Ezra went first, and Rachel died two days after that. My poor mother was strong in spirit but not so strong in body. We buried her beside Ezra and Rachel.

"Need I say that Josephus and Arabella were never the same after that? Their hearts were heavy with sorrow; the memories of their children were everywhere on that small farm. Josephus thought it best to move on and go West, as many people in Tennessee were doing. Some went to this land of Texas, some planned to travel even further to the west, to where the land ended at an ocean called the Pacific.

"The wise men say that the Lord works in mysterious ways, Mr. Fargo. He certainly did where I was concerned. I was what the laws of the land called an orphan, but I was not destined to be alone. Josephus and Arabella Nutbush took me as their own, and I loved them as I had loved my own mother and father.

"On a rainy Sunday morning, Josephus and I loaded the wagon and off we went. Thus would begin the longest journey of my life, one that has continued to this day. But it is here, Mr. Fargo, in Paradise, where my journey will finally end."

"The Danbys?" Fargo asked.

"Yes," Katz said. "The Danbys. It was outside of Little River, in Arkansas, when they set upon us. It happened very quickly. First was a shot, and Josephus *plotzed* right off the buckboard. The Danbys came on us and shot me here"— Katz tapped a spot above his breastbone—"and here." He slapped his left leg. "For good measure, they kicked me a few times, just for fun. Then they went for Arabella."

Katz's eyes misted over. He blinked a few times and the mist was gone. His eyes were cold granite. He said, "Poor Arabella. The truth be told, the woman wasn't exactly a feast on the eyes. God forbid that should stop the Danbys, though. They were drunk on whiskey. They dragged her into the woods and had their way with her, all of those filthy bastards. Her screams will haunt me until the day I die, Skye Fargo, but that wasn't the worst of it.

"There was one of them I remember the best, and I'll tell you why. He was young, maybe, fifteen, sixteen. A little *pisher*. The others, they were older, but they answered to him. They said, 'C'mon, Hoke, take your turn, boy. This lady shore is a fine piece o' meat.'" A bitterness took over his voice. "This Hoke, he smiled at me—that *pisher* smiled at me. He went, but he didn't take his turn with poor Arabella, that wasn't his pleasure. What he did, he shot her three times. So much blood, you shouldn't know. At that point it was almost a mercy, except for one thing: When he shot her, he laughed. Hoke Danby, he laughed just like the Cossack in Lithuania laughed when he killed my father. To people like them, killing is funny. Me, I don't find it so amusing.

"The Danbys left me for dead," Katz went on. "To speak

the truth, I wished I was. Some strangers came along, nice people. From Missouri. They helped me get better. Stronger. I lived, because it was God's will that I live. God has a plan for each of us, Mr. Fargo. In America, they call it destiny. Every man has one. My destiny is to rid the world of every Danby on His green earth. What do you think about that, sir?"

Fargo said, "I ain't a man who argues with noble destinies, Mr. Katz."

"As long as we understand each other," Katz said. "I came to Paradise for one reason and one reason only: to kill every last Danby that I can. And their bastard relatives. No taking prisoners, no trials, nothing. We shoot as many as we can until, God forbid, they shoot us."

"There may be a couple of minor legal problems in your plan, Mr. Katz," Fargo said.

"I answer only to the laws of the Almighty," Katz replied. "And if you're a smart man, which I hear you are, you'll do the same. The Danbys are an abomination to God, Mr. Fargo. They must be destroyed if everlasting peace is to be maintained."

"You sound like a Baptist preacher," Fargo quipped.

Katz smiled a little and said, "I've worshipped among the Baptists. A man could do worse. But me isn't what's important now, Skye Fargo. It's you. You shed their blood, and for the best of all reasons."

"My reasons were purely financial," Fargo said.

"Maybe then," Katz said. "But not now. I have it on very good authority, Mr. Fargo, that the Danbys are coming to Paradise just to make the pleasure of your acquaintance."

"So I've heard," Fargo said.

"I'm here to help," Katz said.

"What if I don't want any help?" Fargo asked.

"Take your blessings where you can," Katz said. "I don't come this way often."

"Word is," Fargo said, "the Danbys are gonna try to

fetch their baby brother first, over to Mineral Springs. Maybe they'll be stopped there."

"Don't treat me like a *shmuck*, Fargo," Katz said. "Mineral Springs is gone already. We both know it. And we both know the Danbys will be here in two days."

"Yeah," Fargo said. "Them's was my calculations, too."

"You don't strike me as a man who runs from trouble, sir," Katz said. "Am I correct in my assumption?"

"I ain't never run from any trouble in my life," Fargo said. "And I've had plenty."

"But the Danbys—do they scare you?"

Fargo said, "The truth? Yeah, they scare me. Right down to my socks."

"Good," Katz said. "You'd be lost to feel any other way. But you won't run, will you?"

Fargo shook his head. He said, "No, I ain't runnin' anywheres."

"Then maybe we should start making a plan, you think?"

"A plan would be nice," Fargo agreed. "I reckon we ought to alert the town council, too. The people of Paradise got a right to know. This is gonna be very bad, ain't it?"

Gunther Toody burst through the swinging kitchen doors with a tray laden with food that filled the air with the sweet-smelling aroma of chicken-fried steak and thick gravy. He slapped Fargo's supper down in front of him and gently placed a plate of chicken—boiled six minutes, with the skin peeled off—in front of Nashville Katz. Fargo tore into his beefsteak and mopped up gravy with a biscuit.

"You eat this every day?" Katz asked him.

"What?" Fargo asked. "Beefsteak?"

"Whatever it is you're enjoying so much," Katz said.

"Then it's beefsteak," Fargo said. "And I eat it as often as I can."

"Look at it," Katz said, prodding his fork into the

stringy, tough slab of beef on Fargo's plate. "All gristle. Not healthy at all."

"You pick your poison, mister, and I'll pick mine," Fargo said, devouring his dinner.

"I think we both picked it, Mr. Fargo," Katz replied with a grimace.

"Surrounded by a passel of the meanest Mishagossie braves we was, me and Hezekiah Jackson—Eyeball Eatin' Jackson to you," Buzzy was saying to Dexter, who was furiously writing down ever word. "You ever heard tell of Eyeball Eatin' Jackson?"

"I don't think so," Dexter said, wide-eyed.

Buzzy was keeping Dexter company in Dexter's room at the boarding house. He was feeling much better today, due in no small part to Ma's tender loving care and in much larger part to the laudanum Prudie spoon-fed him thrice daily. Earlier that morning, Buzzy had gone over to the mercantile and picked up some writing pencils and some paper, at Dexter's request.

"Hezekiah hated injuns, 'specially the Mishagossie. The Cheyenne Sioux, they wasn't so bad. But the Mishagossie were a rough bunch," Buzzy said. "So after Hezekiah kilt himself one, what he'd do was, he'd cut out the redskin's eyeballs an' eat 'em. That's why ever'one called him Eyeball Eatin' Jackson."

"He *ate* their *eyeballs?*" Dexter asked in astonishment. "Actually ate them? That's disgusting," Dexter said. No one back home would ever believe it, much less anyone at Livermore and Beedle. Nevertheless, Dexter continued writing down Buzzy's every word. "Is that what they call . . . cannibalism?"

"Cannibalism?" Buzzy asked, looking puzzled.

"You know," Dexter said. "When people . . . eat other people. Like when they're hungry and there's nothing else to eat."

"Hezekiah, he didn't eat eyeballs 'cause he was hungry," Buzzy explained. "He done it so's the other Injuns would become a-feared of him. See, what a Mishagossie believes is, when he dies, he enters the spirit world of his ancestors. But if he ain't got no eyes, he's damned to spend his hereafter wandering twixt the winds. Sounds kinda loco, I know, but I guess a creature's got a right to believe whatever he's of a mind to."

"I guess," Dexter said.

"We was up in Wyoming Territory, Hezekiah and me, trappin' beaver and coon to take us some skins down to market in Medicine Bow. Was a Mishagossie chief, mean ol' bastard."

"Mis-ha-gossie?" Dexter said. "What kind of tribe are they?"

"You wanna hear this story or not?" Buzzy asked.

"Yes, I'm sorry," Dexter said, and got ready to write again. "So you were on a ridge, you and Mr. Eyeball, and that's when—"

"You ain't got anything like a bottle around here, do ye?" Buzzy asked. "Yarnin' gives me a powerful thirst."

"You mean whiskey?" Dexter asked.

"I don't mean sarsparilla," Buzzy said.

"I don't think so," Dexter said. "Would you like some of this?" He reached over to the night table next to the bed and picked the blue laudanum bottle.

Buzzy's eyes lit up. He took the bottle and uncorked it with his teeth. He took a healthy swig and swallowed. He felt a pleasant warmth in his belly. He said, "Do got a nice kick to it, don't it?" He helped himself to another, then another after that.

"So then what happened?" Dexter asked.

"About what?"

"The ridge," Dexter said. "What happened on the ridge?"

"What ridge?" Buzzy asked, wiping his mouth on a dirty sleeve. He swigged more laudanum.

"The ridge where you were trapped," Dexter asked.

"What trap?"

"The trap on the ridge," Dexter said, getting flustered. "With Eyeball Eatin' Jackson."

"Old Hezekiah? What about him?"

"I don't know," Dexter said. "It's your story."

"It is?" Buzzy asked, as befuddled as Dexter was now. "How's it end?"

"I was hoping *you* knew," Dexter said. First Fargo and now Buzzy Oathammer. Were all storytellers this difficult? Dexter was beginning to think he'd chosen the wrong profession. The last ten days had been one very painful catastrophe after another, between the arduous journey west, the starvation, and getting himself stuffed into a piano. Maybe it was time to go home and find a job that didn't hurt.

A minute or so later, by the time Buzzy had polished off the last of the laudanum, it was noon. Like clockwork, Prudie came through the doorway carrying a tray loaded down with lunch, a plate covered with a napkin, some bread, and a big glass of buttermilk.

"Are you filling this poor boy's head with your wild stories, Buzzy?" Prudie asked.

"I was trying to," Buzzy said, clutching the laudanum bottle. "I think we got sorta sidetracked."

Prudie set the tray down on Dexter's lap, just close enough for Dexter to catch a whiff of her. Prudie smelled of sweet soap and talcum powder. His manhood immediately hardened up and stood at attention. The tray rose an inch or two higher.

Prudie grabbed the empty laudanum bottle from Buzzy, saying, "It's no wonder, drinkin' up all this poor boy's medicine."

Dexter, pushing the tray back down to conceal the bulge under the blanket, said, "It's okay, Miss Prudie. I offered it."

"That's fine," Prudie said to Dexter. "I'll be the one who has to fetch another bottle from Doc Phipps."

"Oh, well, I wouldn't—" Dexter said.

Prudie said to him, "You hush up now, Mr. Dexter Tritt. How do you expect to get better if you don't start eating regular?"

She yanked the starched napkin off the plate, uncovering two large sunny-side up eggs. Dexter grabbed the fork and licked his lips in anticipation. He hadn't had any nice eggs since leaving Brooklyn, New York.

Bringing it to his lips, Buzzy happily blurted out, "Now I remember—Eyeball Eatin' Jackson!"

Dexter looked down at the eggs and saw two steaming yellow eyeballs. His appetite fainted dead away. He grabbed the napkin and covered the plate.

Prudie turned to Buzzy, "Mr. Fargo wants to see you down at the marshal's office. He said to get down there drunk or sober, he didn't say why. Rumor around town is, Paradise's maybe got itself some trouble."

Buzzy was up and going out the door when he said, "I think I know where that trouble's a-comin' from, and I ain't too surprised. Where Skye Fargo goes, trouble tends to follow." He tipped his battered hat at Prudie and said, "See you, ma'am. See you, Dexter."

When he was gone, Prudie snapped at Dexter, "You gonna eat your lunch or do I have to take you over my knee and give you a good spanking."

Dexter could think of worse things, but he dutifully grabbed a piece of bread and started munching, taking a sip of buttermilk now and then. It was hard to eat around Prudie—she excited him too much and food was a poor substitute. But he did his best.

As Dexter tried to eat, Prudie sat on the edge of the bed and grabbed his writing paper. She read, "*His bravery knowing no bounds, the intrepid Buzzy Oathammer fought his way through the deadly throng of bloodthirsty redskin savages, brandishing knife and gun in a devastating display of weaponry, shooting and slashing scores of rampaging redskins."*

She asked Dexter, "You wouldn't be apt to believing anything Buzzy Oathammer spouts, would you?"

"Well, it did sound interesting," Dexter said.

As if confirming his own doubts, Prudie crumpled up the piece of paper and tossed the fruits of Dexter's labor into the small ash can next to the door. She said, "Why do you want to write terrible things like this? You want to put this paper to good use, Dexter Tritt, you write your mother a letter. I bet you ain't wrote her a word since you left New York."

This was almost true. Dexter had written her two letters since leaving home, but he'd written and mailed both of them from Philadelphia, a scant ninety miles from home, the same day he left. But there had been no letters home since then. Somehow, there hadn't been the time to write.

He went to grab the paper from Prudie. She pushed him back onto the pillows, saying, "Those eggs ain't for decoration. You eat 'em, and I'll write the letter." She snatched the pencil and put it to the paper. "Just tell me what you want to say."

Dexter tried to push the vision of eyeballs from his brain and started in on the eggs. All in all, they tasted pretty good. He said, "Okay. I'll do what they call 'dic-tating'."

"I don't know what that means, Mr. Tritt," Prudie said, "but if you dick-tate on me I'll blast you into the middle of next week."

Dexter got red-faced and stammered, "Oh, no, Miss Prudie, nothing like that. What I meant was, I talk and you write down what I say. Can you do that?"

"You ain't the only one who's ever had any schoolin', mister," Prudie said.

"Sorry," Dexter said. He chewed his lunch and began, "Dear Mother. Hope you are well, and I hope Harvey is well as well."

Prudie scribbled the words on the paper. Dexter continued, "I am well, too. Texas is very big and very hot. But the people have been very nice to me. Well, most of them anyway."

Prudie grinned a little and went on writing. Dexter tried to concentrate on what to say in the letter, but Prudie being so near made thinking about anything else extremely difficult. He'd never been so strongly attracted to a woman—any woman—in his life. Her proud, firm breasts were straining against the corset she wore underneath her simple print dress. Prudie would look good in a potato sack, he decided. He couldn't take his eyes off her.

Finally Prudie said, "We ain't gonna get this letter done with you wonderin' what I look like naked."

Dexter got all red-faced at Prudie's remark and stammered, "I wasn't wondering what you . . . I mean, maybe I was . . . but . . . I didn't mean anything by it." He looked down at his plate, the half-eaten eggs cold now, and murmured, "You're very pretty."

"You're sweet," Prudie said. "You got yourself a girlie-girl back home?"

"You mean like a girlfriend?" Dexter asked.

"Yes," Prudie said. "A gal to take walks with, set out on the front porch after supper with, like that. I would think you're real popular with the ladies."

"Popular? Me?" Dexter asked. "You're teasing me now, aren't you?"

Prudie said, "I ain't the teasin' type, Mr. Tritt. All I'm sayin' is, you ain't a bad-looking young man. A little scrawny—you could use a good ten pounds of meat on your bones—but that aside, you ain't too hard to look at it. Polite, too, which you don't see much in these parts. I imagine there's lots of gals would be lucky to have you."

"That's kind of you to say, Miss Prudie," Dexter said. "But to answer your question, I don't have a girl. But I bet you have lots of boyfriends."

"Some," Prudie said. "I see Purvis Mayhew sometimes. He's the son of Thaddeus Mayhew, owns the Circle-T Ranch north of town. And sometimes I walk home from church with Horatio Primm. He works for Mr. Muckle at the mercantile. But I don't think I love either of 'em or anything." Then she asked him, "Ever kissed a gal? Not includin' your mother."

"Well, it sort of depends," Dexter stammered. "On your definition of kissing. Once, in fifth grade, Bonnie May Klingman let me kiss her on the cheek—"

"No," Prudie said. "What I mean is, you ever kiss a gal on the *mouth*?" She leaned into him, pushed the tray aside, and planted her lips firmly on his. Dexter's heart started hammering in his chest.

Prudie said softly, "It's considered polite when a gal is kissing you to kiss back. I won't bite."

Their lips came together again, and this time Dexter eagerly kissed her back. He wasn't too sure what to do with his hands. He knew what he *wanted* to do with them, but wasn't sure it was proper to start groping her this early in their relationship. He kissed her hard, and Prudie kissed back even harder, until suddenly her tongue was sliding into his mouth. Dexter followed Prudie's lead and slithered his tongue into hers. His manhood sprang to attention and made a blanket tent again.

They kissed hungrily, passionately. Prudie grabbed Dexter's left hand and planted it on her breast. Dexter started sweating, but didn't care.

She pulled away and asked him, "You're a virgin, aren't you?"

"No," he said. "I'm a Protestant."

Prudie said, "What I mean, you ain't never made love to a gal, have you?"

119

"Well," Dexter said, "it all depends—"

"They's only one way to answer the question, Dexter," Prudie said. "If you got to think about it, then you've never done it."

She started unbuttoning the top of her dress. Dexter looked alarmed and said, "But your mother—"

"Me first," Prudie said. She chuckled and added, "Don't worry. Ma's over at Muckle's buying next week's groceries. She sets into gossipin' with her friends, she won't be home for another two hours."

She flipped a few more buttons and squirmed out of the dress. She sat before him and exposed the most stunning pair of breasts Dexter had ever seen. The only breasts he'd ever seen, outside of some on the French postcards he found in one of Harvey's dresser drawers. They were high and firm, sloping gently where they ended enticingly at two round, jutting nipples.

He made a strangled sound deep in his throat, a croak of surprise and intense desire. Prudie said, "You can touch 'em if you want."

Dexter extended his hands, which were shaking uncontrollably, and placed them flat on her firm naked knockers. He wasn't certain what to do next and felt panic creeping in. Fortunately, Prudie took the lead and said, "Put that tray on the floor, Dexter."

He did as instructed. Prudie slid into bed next to him and shed the last of her undergarments, saying, "I think you're supposed to get naked, too, for this to work."

It was really happening, Dexter thought dimly as he pulled off the undershirt and long johns, which were way too warm anyway. He was still bruised and the tender spots were bandaged up, but the important thing was, he was finally going to become a man. There were so many things he wanted to do to Prudie, but he wasn't sure which one to tackle first. Again, Prudie saved him the trouble, rolling on top of him, her firm, plump melons sliding across his bare chest. His throbbing manhood pressed against her shapely thigh. Prudie inched up further atop him until her luscious titties were a mere inch from Dexter's face. She jammed his face into her chest, moaning, "Kiss 'em, Dexter honey. Do whatever you want."

He kissed her tits all over and nibbled eagerly on her nipples, which grew taut to Dexter's loving tongue. Prudie threw her head back and held Dexter by the ears as he kissed and sucked, maneuvering his head from one golden mound to the other. It hurt, but he didn't mind the pain one little bit.

Prudie let go of Dexter's ears and pulled the blankets up over them. She started kissing his chest, working her way south. She ran her tongue down his belly and curled her fingers around his pulsing shaft. Dexter's heart hammered even faster now and the blood pounded in his ears. Prudie took his throbbing member into her sweet mouth and lovingly did things with her tongue he'd scarcely dreamed of. His eyes crossed until he was seeing double as Prudie's head bobbed up and down. She ran her tongue up and down the underside of his pecker, gripping it at the base. Dexter fought like a devil to keep from popping off in her mouth, which wouldn't be proper at all.

Sensing his mounting passion, Prudie rolled onto her back and held her arms out to him, saying, "Now let's send you home with some *nice* memories of Texas."

"Do you do this with lots of men?" Dexter asked.

"No," Prudie replied. "Only the ones I like. And I haven't liked too many."

He climbed on top of her. Prudie took his aching pecker and guided him between her legs. He slid into her warm, moist womanhood and tried not to faint from the pleasure. Prudie wrapped her legs around his and gripped his ass cheeks, forcing him deeply into her.

"Oh, Dexter!" Prudie blurted out excitedly. "Oh, you nasty, nasty boy!" She kissed and licked his ear as he went on pumping her. He buried his face in a pillow and let nature take its course—he had no choice in the matter by this time. He erupted inside her, his cries of ecstasy muffled by the pillow.

"Mummph," he gurgled.

Prudie moaned in unison, holding him tight as he climaxed. When he was done, they lay there, still entwined, catching their breath. Finally, Dexter rolled off of her and said sheepishly, "I'm sorry it . . . ended so soon."

Prudie smiled and kissed him on the mouth. She said, "It's okay, Dexter honey. I hear tell a man's first time is always his quickest. And don't forget, dear, we still have an hour before Mama gets home."

"We do, don't we?" Dexter said, and felt a bit guilty that he wasn't up and out and chasing down Skye Fargo's name on a contract. But not that guilty, not with a beautiful young lady lying buck naked beside him making some sweet overtures.

Two minutes later, Prudie was bouncing up and down on Dexter's stiff member, pressing Dexter's hands on her titties. Suddenly the bedroom door flew open and Dexter heard an audible gasp of shock and surprise.

He looked past Prudie, who was still sitting atop him, and saw Ma Fisher, Fargo, and Marshal Fix standing in the doorway. Ma Fisher looked stricken. Marshal Fix looked embarrassed. Fargo was grinning with the slightest hint of jealousy.

Dexter's shaft fainted dead away.

"Looks like we interrupted something," Fargo said.

"Prudence!" Ma Fisher cried angrily. "Mr. Tritt!"

"Call me Dexter," he said.

"Just what in blazes are you two doing in here?" Ma Fisher demanded.

"Writing a letter?" Dexter asked.

Prudie fumbled with a sheet and wrapped it around her

body. Fargo and Marshal Fix looked away respectfully, though both stole a glance here and there.

"Writing a letter in a pig's ass," Ma Fisher snapped, and grabbed her daughter's left ear. Prudie howled in protest. Ma said, "A fine reputation you're gonna give us in this town! I'm only glad your dear departed father ain't around to see this!"

"Her father died, huh?" Fargo whispered to the marshal.

"Nope," Fix whispered back. "He just departed."

Ma gave Prudie's ear another twist. Prudie wailed and said, "It's ain't what it looks like, Ma. We was just getting acquainted is all."

"Sure, regular kissin' cousins, that's what you are," Ma said. She turned to Fargo and said, "A fine specimen of a man you brought into my home, Skye Fargo! The minute my back is turned, he rapes my daughter!"

"Rape?" Dexter blurted out. This was getting serious.

"Now just hold your water, Ma," the marshal said. "I think we all seen the same thing. And from where I'm standin', I'd have to conclude Prudence weren't being forced against her will."

Ma was not mollified. She pointed an accusing finger at Dexter and said, "Y'all got yourself a choice, Mr. Tritt— you can leave my home through the front door, or I can throw your worthless hide out the window."

She dragged her daughter by the ear out of the bedroom and down the hall, Prudie howling all the way. They heard Ma screaming, ". . . And you'll stay locked in your room till your next birthday! I will not have any uncertified goings-on under my roof!"

Dexter looked devastated. He said, "I did a terrible thing, didn't I?"

"Nothing any man in this county wouldn't have done, given the chance," Marshal Fix said.

Fargo rummaged through the small closet and grabbed Dexter's suitcase, which he tossed onto the bed. Gathering up Dexter's clothes, he said, "Since we only got ten minutes, you best get your britches on."

"Where are we going?" Dexter asked.

"*We* are not going anywhere," Fargo said. "*You* are going home, and today. There's trouble coming, and you'll just get in the way."

"But there's no train out of here for three more days," Dexter said.

"This is true," Fargo said. "That's why Buzzy's taking you in the wagon—north, sixty miles to Galena, where you can catch another train back East.

"But I still haven't finished what I came here to do," Dexter protested, putting on his socks and shoes, unaware that he was still naked as a jaybird. "I told you, Mr. Fargo, what will happen to my job if I don't—"

"They ain't payin' y'all to get killed, son," Fargo said. "I was you, I'd find me another job."

"I don't want another job," Dexter said. "And I don't wanna leave, either. Prudie and me—"

"What about Prudie and you?" Fargo asked.

"I think I love her," Dexter said.

"Yeah, well, that's something you two got to work out for your own selves," Fargo said, looking out the window. "In the meantime, your carriage awaits."

Dexter went to the window. Downstairs, Buzzy was sitting in the buckboard, holding the horses' reins.

Dexter said to Marshal Fix, "I don't have to leave just because Skye Fargo tells me to. That's not legal!"

"No, it's not," Fix said. "But as the law in Paradise, *I'm* ordering you to leave."

"Oh," Dexter said.

Five minutes later Dexter was sitting on the buckboard. Fargo tossed Dexter's suitcase into the back of the wagon. Dexter stared straight ahead, looking lower than a snake's toes, as Buzzy said, "Ought to take two days, maybe three, to Galena, dependin' on the weather. Got us enough food and water for five if need be."

Fargo said to Dexter, "Sorry it had to be this way, friend, but someday you'll thank me. That is, if the Danbys don't kill me first."

Dexter said nothing. From an upstairs window, he saw Prudie watching them. Dexter gave her a little smile. She smiled back and his heart lurched in his chest. It wasn't supposed to end this way, he thought. Dexter had envisioned himself returning home in triumph, with Fargo's signature on the contract and Prudie Fisher on his arm. They'd be very happy, maybe take an apartment on Knickerbocker Street, a few doors down from his mother and Harvey. Livermore and Beedle would give him a big fat raise and a promotion and Dexter Tritt would be the toast of New York City. Life would be good.

Instead, he was going home a complete and utter failure. He'd been tested and was found wanting.

No, it wasn't supposed to end this way. Not for a minute it wasn't.

"I know how you're feeling, son," Fargo said to him. "But look on the bright side. At least you're going home. Eddie Buzzell never got that chance."

Dexter looked at Fargo and said, "Eddie Buzzell died in the line of duty. Eddie Buzzell died doing his job. To my way of thinking, he died a very rich man."

"Don't beat yourself up too much, kid," Fargo said. "Nobody tried as hard as you did. That counts for something. Not every horse can win the first time out of the gate." He stuck his hand out to Dexter. "So long, kid."

Dexter continued staring straight ahead. He said to Buzzy, "If we're going, then let's be on our way."

"Suit yourself," Buzzy said, and snapped the reins. The buckboard lurched down Main Street toward the western end of town. Fargo watched as the buckboard turned a corner and disappeared from view. He might actually miss the skinny little runt somewhat.

Marshal Fix said, "You did the right thing, Fargo, and you know it."

"Of course I know it," Fargo said. "So why do I feel like such a shitheel?"

"No explainin' why some of life's big turds land in your soup," Fix said. "But don't worry, Fargo. Remember the old saying: No good deed ever goes unpunished."

14

Two hours after Dexter and Buzzy rode out of Paradise, a man named Lemuel Dill rode in, looking like death warmed over. He'd ridden hell-bent for leather from Mineral Springs, or what was left of it, two days earlier with but one mission—to alert the territory that the Danbys were headed its way. But judging from the scenes of townspeople loading up their wagons and skedaddling out of town, the news had already leaked out.

Lem Dill was a poor cotton farmer who lived in a ramshackle little house with his wife and three children six miles outside of Mineral Springs. Lem had ridden into town to beg the banker, Wellington Botts, for an extra week to make his note payment, just until he could get his meager crop in. Botts would say no, of course, the heartless bastard. He'd already forced the Calloway and Dingle families off their spreads and was buying up their land for pennies on the dollar.

Lem Dill had ridden into Mineral Springs an hour after the Danbys had all but laid it to waste. Most of the town was smoldering ashes, with lots of folks weeping over the dead and wounded. Inside the bank, one of the few structures in town left standing, Wellington Botts and his idiot son Alexander were already drawing flies. Thanking the Almighty for his personal good fortune, Lemuel Dill stepped outside the bank. A man, his eyes wide in mortal terror, ran up to Lemuel Dill and grabbed his arm. Dill recognized the man as Harley Snow, one of his neighbors.

"Harley," Lem Dill said, "what the hell happened here?"

Harley Snow was half out of his mind. He grabbed Lem Dill by the sleeve of his battered coat and shouted at him, "Was the Danbys done this! Get on your horse, Lemuel, and warn ever'one in the territory. We're counting on you."

Lem Dill rode and warned Brazos and Boonsville and Prairie Point before riding into Paradise. The Danbys were nowhere to be seen.

Dill dismounted in front of the town marshal's office, but the place was empty. He asked some jasper who was packing up a wagon, "Where can I find your local lawman?"

"Over to the church most likely," the jasper said, tossing bundles into the wagon bed.

Lem Dill asked, "Where's everyone going?"

"Ain't you heard?" the jasper said. "The Danby clan is coming to Paradise, and this town ain't safe for man nor beast. Some of the fools are talkin' about taking them on. But not us—me and the missus and the young'uns are clearing out till this blows over. If you're smart, mister, you'll do the same."

Lem Dill made his way over to the church. Inside twenty or so of the townsfolk were arguing loudly with each other; it was only a matter of minutes before full-blown panic would set in. On the dais, a man of the cloth was banging his fist on the pulpit and yelling for them to sit down and shut up. Beside the reverend was an older, slightly hunched-over and paunchy man with salt-and-pepper hair. He had a tin star pinned to his vest. There were a couple of other men on the pulpit as well.

Marshal Edwin Fix said to the congregation, "The facts as we know 'em are this: The Danbys are comin' to Paradise and no mistake. Mr. Fargo and Mr. Katz and I have decided to make a stand agin 'em, defend Paradise. Anyone wants to join us is more than welcome."

Wilbur Muckle served as the acting mayor of Paradise. As the owner of the town mercantile he was a good businessman but a lousy mayor. But the mayor he was, mostly because nobody else wanted the job.

"What about it, Muckle?" Jacob Newcastle, a rancher on the north end of town, wanted to know. "The Danbys comin' or ain't they? And if they do, what do y'all plan on doing about it?"

Wilbur Muckle wiped his sweaty brow with a hanky and said, "We're doing everything we can, Jacob."

I strongly suggest we bow our heads in prayer and beg God's everlasting mercy . . ." Reverend Micah Hackleberry suggested. He was greeted with a chorus of jeers, one man saying, "Save it for Sunday, Reverend!"

"Maybe they ain't comin'," said Bertrand Lingle, who owned the bakery. "We don't even know where they are."

A new round of arguments erupted, and Lemuel Dill found himself yelling above the crowd, "I know where the Danbys are!"

That got their attention. The church fell silent and all eyes turned to him. Marshal Fix said, "Don't believe I recognize you, stranger."

"Name's Lem Dill, from Mineral Springs," Dill said. "Or whatever's left of it. The Danbys left a mess of death and hurtin' there a couple of days ago. I seen 'em this mornin'—they're holed up about twelve, fifteen miles from here, over at Cherry Creek."

"You sure it were the Danbys?" Fix asked.

"Sure as I'm standin' here," Dill said. "They ain't exactly makin' no effort to hide themselves."

Fargo said to the marshal, "Cherry Creek is north. Maybe we should mosey on up and take us a little look-see. Maybe we'll even get lucky and take 'em by surprise, blast a few and take their number down." He turned to Nashville

Katz and asked, "Reckon you'd care to tag along, Nashville?"

"Does a bear shit in the woods?" he responded.

"I'll go with y'all," Fix said. "Might need me."

"With all due respect, Edwin," Fargo said, "I think you'd do Paradise a hell of a lot more good if you stayed here and rounded up every able-bodied man who can hit the broad side of a barn."

Edwin Fix was as tough as any lawman who'd been paid to keep the peace in any number of small Texas towns, but the truth was, he was a little older and a little more tired than this particular job demanded—and he was the first to admit it. He did not protest all that much.

"All right, Fargo," Fix said. "You and Mr. Katz here do just that, and for corn's sake be careful."

"You think we're maybe planning on being careless?" Katz wanted to know.

"What do we all do till you get back?" Wilbur Muckle asked.

"Turn some wagons on their sides to use as cover, then use whatever you can find to use for any extra shelter," Fargo said. "Then hope for the best."

"But expect the worst," Katz added.

They went to the livery stable to fetch their horses. On the street, Danby fever was still sweeping Paradise. Katz looked up at the sky, which was thickening with rain clouds, and commented, "I don't know if I like the look of that sky."

Fargo looked up and said, "Looks fine to me. If we're lucky, won't be no moon tonight."

"Don't you think that might make it hard for us to spot the Danbys?"

"Probably," Fargo said, "but it'll be hard for the Danbys to spot us, too."

"Such a smart man," Katz said as they mounted up. "Have you always been this smart, Mr. Fargo?"

"I get by," he said, and they rode hard out of town and into the longest night either of them would ever know.

The first thing they saw was Dexter and Buzzy hanging upside down from a walnut tree.

"What the hell are *they* doing here?" Fargo said.

Next to him, laying flat on his belly, Katz observed, "To turn down an invitation from the Danbys is never an option. This is not a goodness."

Dexter and Buzzy had their hands bound behind their backs. They hung suspended six inches or so off the ground. Their ankles were also bound. The Danbys took turns swinging them back and forth in drunken delight. It was hard to tell if they were dead or alive.

Fargo and Katz were well hidden under a brush-covered ridge maybe a thousand yards from where the gang was camped by the creek in a mess of walnut trees. The campfire was blazing; as Lem Dill had claimed, they were taking no pains to conceal themselves.

"I send him out of town to protect him, and he sticks his nose in the biggest hornet's nest we got," Fargo said. He scrambled to his feet and said, "I got to get to 'em—"

Katz grabbed Fargo's arm and pulled him back down, saying, "Are you planning your own funeral? How far do you think you'll get?"

"Then let's get in a little closer and start blasting," Fargo said, and was up again.

"Wait, please," Katz said, pulling him back. "I think I have a better idea."

"Will I like it?" Fargo asked.

"If it works, you'll like it," Katz said. "If it doesn't, probably not so much."

"Well, you come West to get yourself a story," Buzzy said to Dexter. "I'd say you done got yourself a pip."

Dexter had a nasty headache from hanging upside down,

131

and the rope binding his wrists was cutting off important blood flow to his hands. They swayed gently like two pendulums, while the Danbys and their kin drank large amounts of whiskey and became increasingly meaner as the night—and the whiskey—wore on.

After the joyous act of "losing his cherry" (as the boys in Brooklyn so gently referred to it) that morning, Dexter's day had gone straight to hell. He'd been forced to leave the girl he loved, chased out of town, and then things really went downhill.

The Danbys had caught them with their pants down— literally in Dexter's case. They'd passed a peach tree six or so miles out of town and had eaten their fill. Not long after, Dexter, who was not accustomed to such fresh fruit, felt the need to answer the call of nature. Badly.

"Warned ya not to eat so many of them peaches," Buzzy said as he jerked the reins and brought the horses to a halt. "They taste sweet, but run through ya like lightning."

Dexter was squatting over some shrubbery doing his business when he felt the cool touch of gunmetal on the back of his neck. A voice behind him shouted out, "Stand and deliver!"

"I can maybe deliver," Dexter said, "but standing may be a problem."

The voice said, "Then you oughta know, stranger, them bushes you're crappin' in is poison ivy. Your butt's gonna get all swole and itchy in 'bout an hour."

Dexter felt like crying. He said, "I guess asking for some privacy is out of the question."

"Git up," the voice said.

One very mean-looking man appeared in front of him, then another, then a few more behind them. Some were bearded, some had moustaches, but they all had one thing in common—they were trail dirty and had the look of men who'd slaughter a man for the shoes on his feet. Dexter stood and gingerly hitched up his pants, the gun barrel still on his neck. He saw Buzzy, hands on top of his head, coming his way. Two more men were walking behind him, shoving him along with the barrels of their rifles. Some other men rummaged through the stuff on the buckboard, breaking open his battered suitcase and tossing his clothes all over the place. One of the men flung the pages of his adventure yarn, *Big Timmy Thompson: Scourge of the Pecos,* into the wind, scattering paper everywhere. Dexter had labored three weeks on it before coming to Texas.

"Nothing but a bunch of stinky clothes in this 'un, Hoke," one of them said.

The one called Hoke emerged from the trees, followed by a smaller man Dexter realized wasn't a man at all, but a girl. A pretty girl, he saw, despite the trail dust and ill-fitting men's britches. Her face was almost concealed by the beat-up ten gallon hat. Despite her good looks, she didn't look any less mean than some of the men. This was confirmed when she said to the one named Hoke, "They ain't got diddly. Let's plug 'em and be on our way."

"Yeah, Hoke," said one of the men. "Time's a wastin'."

Hoke said to Dexter, "Y'all got any money?"

Dexter glanced nervously over at Buzzy, who didn't look happy at all. He said to Dexter, "Best give 'em what you got, boy."

"All of it?" Dexter asked.

"It's the Danbys, for corn's sake!" Buzzy snapped. "Give him the damn money."

The dreaded Danby Gang. Dexter suddenly felt dizzy, like he was going to pass out. He reached into his pocket and pulled out some bills and coins, about thirty dollars give or take. He handed it to Hoke. Hoke took it and tossed it over his shoulder, where it scattered like Dexter's pages. Hoke said, "Divvy it up, boys."

Some of the men pounced on it, clawing and grabbing

133

and fighting. It was, Dexter thought, the most undignified spectacle he'd ever witnessed.

While the men were otherwise occupied, the girl said to Hoke, "We kill 'em now?"

"Yeah, okay," Hoke said.

The girl grinned from ear to ear like a starving wolf pouncing on a rabbit. She reached for the pistol in her holster when Hoke called out, "Which one of you onionheads wants to drill these here jaspers?"

The merry band of cutthroats all raised their hands, shouting, "Me, Hoke . . . I'll do it, Hoke . . . it's my turn, Hoke . . . Ah'll ventilate the sidewinders, Hoke . . ."

"You said it was *my* turn," the girl said, and got all pouty.

"I never said such, Violet," Hoke said.

They started bickering like an old married couple until Violet said something about Hoke's teeny-weeny little pecker and he backhanded her hard, knocking her flat on her ass.

He said to her, "Now go fix us a mess of beans and bacon, you wicked slut. I don't git my supper in ten minutes, I'll punch your heart out."

Violet got all pouty and stomped off back to camp. One of the men asked Hoke, "What about them?"

"Yeah, Hoke," another said. "You said we could kill 'em."

"Shut your traps, all y'all," Hoke thundered. "We got us some hard work to do in Paradise tomorrow, and I been noticin' y'all's shootin' got real sloppy." He looked over at Buzzy and Dexter. "String 'em up by their ankles. First I'm a-gonna have my supper, then you slobs are gonna have yourselves a little target practice."

Madder than blazes, he stomped off toward camp. The subject was closed.

One of the men said to Dexter, "Hoke's a bear when he's hungry."

Now, a little later, here he was, hanging upside down from a tree, a guest of the deadliest outlaw gangs the West had to offer. It seemed highly probable he'd be sharing the same fate as his predecessor Eddie Buzzell.

"Are they really going to use us for target practice?" Dexter asked Buzzy.

"Don't bet against it," Buzzy said. "You best start sayin' yer prayers, son. I'd say mine, but I never learnt any. Pray they get so boozed up they can't hit the broad side of anything."

Given the circumstances, Dexter did just that. Then he heard Hoke Danby, who was sitting by the campfire guzzling a bottle of hooch, say, "All right, boys. Line up and start blasting. Whoever misses don't get no more whiskey tonight."

The Danbys and Gorches and Gribbles toddled drunkenly over to where Dexter and Buzzy were swaying lazily from the cottonwood, clamoring for the best spot and loading their pistols. They were standing maybe twenty feet away, a little too close for comfort.

"You first, Earl. You're the sloppiest of this bunch." Hoke teased.

Earl was weaving slightly, which didn't make his task much easier. He squeezed one eye shut, aimed, and fired. His shot kicked up some dust a foot from Dexter's head."

"You lose, little brother," Hoke said. Earl cursed and skulked away. "Nathan—you next."

Nathan Gribble aimed and fired. Like the others, he was feeling no pain. He saw two Dexters and two Buzzys hanging, and fired a shot at them, figuring with four instead of two he was bound to hit something. Instead, the bullet whizzed directly between them and slammed into a gnarly old oak.

"You couldn't hit a turd stain on a bedsheet, Nathan," Jeeter Gorch squealed.

Nathan took great exception to this and lunged at

Jeeter. They fell backward and started rolling around in the dirt, pummeling each other. Hoke yelled for his brother Chigger to go next. Unlike the others, Chigger was cold sober.

Chigger took his time, aiming the pistol straight at Dexter's head. Dexter closed his eyes and waited to die.

A cry filled the still night. "Helloooo the camp! Helloooo the camp!"

Like lightening, ten members of the Danby Gang whirled around and pointed their guns at the sound. No one was more surprised than Dexter to see Nashville Katz push through some shrubs and saunter into the encampment as if he hadn't a care in the world. His clothes were all ripped and dirty.

" 'Twas a wise man who said, 'Jesus Saves!'," Katz bellowed. "But it 'twas a wiser man who said, 'Yes, but Moses invests!' "

"Who the hell are you?" Lyle Gorch asked.

"I can't likely recollect," Katz said, sounding very much like a Texan and not the Easterner he was. "But what's in a name, my very good friend? I've been wandering this prairie for ten years looking for my long-lost Ethel—Ethel Toffelmeyer. Kidnapped by a band of Comanche, the bloodthirsty savages!"

Katz dove onto the ground and started growling deep in his throat, rubbing his face in the dirt and kicking his arms and legs like a kid having a temper tantrum. He got onto all fours and started scratching his armpit like a flea-bitten mongrel, then scampered over to a patch of grass and started pulling it out and stuffing it into his mouth. He had the gang's attention.

"He's plum loco," Jeeter Gorch said.

"Madder'n a shithouse rat," Earl Danby agreed.

"Mad am I?" Katz cried now. "I'll show you mad!" He started banging his head against the live oak and started spouting all kinds of gibberish. He hugged the tree and said, "Oh, my darling Ethel, I've finally found you!"

"Somebody put him outta his misery," Hoke said.

"No, Hoke," Violet said. "It's bad luck to kill a crazy man."

"Yes, put me out of my misery!" Katz said, and pulled a pistol from his belt. He put the barrel up to his forehead, saying, "You betrayed me, Ethel, with a redskin! Good-bye, cruel world!"

He cocked the pistol and put it to his head, looking for all the world like a man about to blow his head off, when Packy Gribble said, "Don't do it, mister! Ethel ain't worth it."

"You know," Katz said, "you're right. She isn't." He trained the gun on Packy and shot him twice in the chest. He whirled and fired at Lyle Gorch, putting two well-placed shots into Lyle's heart. Earl and Jeeter Gorch each fired off a shot, both of which went wild. Katz hit the ground and scrambled away into the night. Hoke was up and clearing leather when two rifle shots pierced the night and hit the ground inches from his feet.

"Ambush!" someone shouted.

"Mind the horses, Violet," Hoke bellowed. Then all hell broke loose.

Fargo cursed and jammed another shell into the chamber of the Henry. He'd missed completely. He made his way further down the ridge, hunkered down, and fired again. He saw someone go down and not get up and prayed it wasn't anyone he knew. The others were predictably fanning out on either side of Fargo's position, firing blindly. The moon had gone behind some clouds, giving Fargo the chance to hustle farther down the ridge

Down in the camp, Dexter asked Buzzy, "Are we dead yet?"

Buzzy said, "What's yer rush?"

Nashville Katz came out of nowhere, as stealthily as he'd disappeared, and started slicing frantically through Dexter's ropes. He severed them, and Dexter's head hit the ground with a painful clunk. Katz went to work on Buzzy's ropes as Dexter tried to shake his head clear. Buzzy thudded to the ground and said to Katz, "Mister Nashville, words just cain't express my appreciation."

"We're not home yet, thank you very much," Katz said, undoing Dexter's wrists, then Buzzy's. He grabbed a groggy Dexter by the collar and the seat of the pants and hustled him away, Buzzy right behind. The firefight had started in earnest now, and gun smoke filled the air.

Fargo stole his way down to where the Danbys' horses were corralled. While the others were busy shooting at anything that moved behind him, Fargo pulled the ropes off the trees and started shooing the horses away. The frightened beasts galloped off into the night. Fargo felt something very hard crash down on his skull and dropped to his knees, dazed. Someone jumped on him from behind and wrapped one arm around his neck. The other arm clutched a very long, very sharp pigsticker and clearly intended to plunge it into anything fleshy. Fargo elbowed the man in the chest and felt titty. Violet Danby grunted and fell backward, releasing her grip. Before he could get control of his senses, she dived at him again and stuck him deeply in the upper thigh.

Enraged, Fargo reached up and grabbed her arms and flung her over his head. Violet was airborne for a second, then hit the ground. Fargo was up and clearing leather, blood squirting out of the wound on his leg. Violet scrambled over to her knife and grabbed it. Fargo kicked it out of her hand, then and pointed the Colt at her.

"You wouldn't shoot a woman, would you?" she said.

He'd been forced to do worse, but still preferred not to. Instead, he kicked her in the head as hard as he could. Violet saw beautiful stars and toppled over sideways, then lay still.

Dexter, only vaguely aware of what was happening due to delayed shock, felt himself being propelled through the darkness and thrown over the rear end of a horse. Then they were moving, the warm breeze in his face. Shots rang out behind them, and then Dexter saw Fargo and Buzzy Oathammer on the Ovaros, galloping up alongside them.

"Hang on tight, young feller," Buzzy bellowed as Fargo spurred the Ovaro to greater speed.

Katz managed to keep pace as the gunshots faded into the distance. The Danbys' horses were scattered all over, and that would buy Fargo and the others some sorely needed time. Katz veered his horse to the left to avoid hitting a tree stump, then snapped spurs to flanks and rode up even with Fargo and his passenger.

As he did, he heard Fargo yell at him, "You done lost your cargo, Nashville!"

Katz stole a look behind and sure enough, Dexter was nowhere to be seen. "Now where did he go, that stupid-head kid?" he groused, and jerked the horse to an abrupt halt. He didn't have long to wait. Dexter came charging through the scrub, arms and legs pumping, and he wasn't alone. Behind him, in hot pursuit, spraying pig snot over half of West Texas, was the biggest, ugliest, and most ornery wild boar Katz had ever seen.

"Faster, Mr. Tritt, faster! That isn't a ham sandwich behind you," Katz urged, going for his pistol. He couldn't get a clear shot at the wild boar without hitting Dexter.

"What's chasing me?" Dexter wailed in mortal terror. *"What the hell is chasing me?"*

Gasping for breath and running for his life, Dexter moved, but not fast enough. The wild boar's snout, little horns and all, connected with his backside, sending him hurtling forward. Dexter yelped in pain, but remained on his feet, running even faster, heading straight for Katz's horse.

Katz's eyes widened in alarm as Dexter hurled himself toward the horse, arms pinwheeling as he tried to keep his balance. Katz cried out, waving his arms wildly, "Go the other way, Dexter, to the left. To the left!"

Dexter barely heard, running on sheer panic now, as the boar tried to gore him a second time. Before Katz could get out of the way, Dexter barreled straight at them. The horse reared up in fear, sending Katz flying ass backward. He hit the ground hard, getting the wind knocked out of him.

While Dexter was off somewhere screaming, Katz caught his breath and lifted his face up. He saw the wild boar two feet from his face. The boar was snorting angrily, his merciless, cunning black eyes glistening in the faint moonlight. Katz fumbled for his gun and the boar charged. Katz vainly tried to roll away, but he knew he was as good as dead.

Two shots rang out. The boar squealed pitifully and dropped like the town drunk on Saturday night. A few yards away, Fargo sat atop the Ovaro and holstered his Colt.

"Pretty fair shootin', Fargo," Buzzy said, and hopped off the horse to find Dexter.

"Did you kill it?" Katz asked, still afraid to open his eyes.

"Yup," Fargo said. "Pretty stupid way to die for a man who ain't allowed to eat pork, don't you think?

"In Texas," Nashville Katz declared, standing up and dusting himself off, "there are more stupid ways to die than hairs on your head."

"He's over here," they heard Buzzy say, and made their way over. Dexter was lying on his side, rubbing his very sore and swollen backside. Jeeter Gorch had been right.

Dexter gazed up at them. He looked like a lot of things—

hurt, scared half out of his mind, bewildered. But mostly what he looked like was exhausted.

"Are we going home now, Mama?" he asked no one in particular.

"Boy, is this kid lost," Buzzy said.

"We'll all be if we don't make tracks," Fargo said. "Won't be long before the Danbys nab their horses. Let's get this boy situated."

Together they lifted Dexter up. Fargo said, "I best take him from here. He's my cross to bear, I reckon."

They eased Dexter down onto the back of the Ovaro. "Gently, boys," Buzzy said as they got him onto the saddle. "Dexter here done shit in a patch of poison ivy."

"I wanna go home now, Mama," Dexter said listlessly. "When are we going home?"

"Now," Fargo said, mounting the Ovaro. "We're all going home now, boy."

They went home, dragging their weary asses into Paradise just as the first rays of sun poked their way through an overcast sky. The town was deserted. Main Street looked like the aftermath of a riot, and the Danbys hadn't even shown up yet. Edwin Fix was sitting in front of the jail on the wood-plank sidewalk in a rickety old chair, serenely smoking his pipe.

As they trotted up, Marshal Fix glanced up at them and saw the dried blood on Fargo's pants. He said, "Looks like you found 'em."

"They found us," Fargo said, dismounting. The others did the same, then helped Dexter down. He stood, but unsteadily.

Fargo looked around. "Did anybody stay behind to fight?"

"Some of the men wanted to," Fix said, "but their wives wouldn't let 'em."

"Isn't that always the case?" Katz said, sounding slightly disgusted.

"How soon before they get here?" Fix asked.

"An hour, maybe sooner," Fargo said.

"Don't give us much time, do it?" Fix fiddled with his pipe, tamping down the tobacco. "Hardly seems worth it though."

"You can all go if you want to," Katz said. "I'm staying."

"What fer? Ain't nothing left to defend," Fix said. "My understandin' of the law's always been, you need people around to obey it, else it don't work too well."

"You have your laws, Marshal, and that's a niceness," Katz said. "Me, I answer to a higher authority."

"Yeah," Fargo said wearily, "and as we all know, I got to stay and fight the Danbys, too." He turned to Buzzy. "What about you, old timer?"

"Old timer," Buzzy grumbled. "I'll dance on your grave, whippersnapper." He spit in the dirt. "Paradise has been pretty good to me, all things bein' equal. Guess I'm obliged to stay."

"Hell's bells," the marshal said, smiling a little and looking ten years younger. He jumped out of the chair and pulled his six-guns from his holster. "Glad to know there's still a few pairs of balls left in this territory."

"What about him?" Katz asked, motioning to Dexter, who looked like something the cat had dragged in.

"Where can we stash him so's he don't get killed, Edwin?" Fargo asked.

"There's a tornado cellar behind Muckle's mercantile," Fix said. "Good a place as any."

Fargo and Buzzy each grabbed one of Dexter's arms and half-walked, half-dragged him toward the mercantile. Dexter said, "Where are we going?"

"Someplace you'll be safe till this shitstorm blows over," Fargo said.

"I don't want to be someplace safe," Dexter pleaded. "I want to help."

"Best way to help us is by stayin' out of the way," Fargo said.

They escorted Dexter to the back of the mercantile. Fargo opened the door to the storm cellar. Six splintery wooden steps led down to a hollowed out hole in the ground.

"Get down there," Fargo said to Dexter.

"Please, Mr. Fargo," Dexter said. "Let me stay with you. Maybe I can—"

Fargo placed his hand flat on Dexter's chest and pushed him backward. Dexter fell the few feet to the bottom of the storm cellar, stunned but not any worse for wear. Fargo said to him, "You got laid and you've been banished, robbed, tortured, shot at, and gotten chased by a wild pig. I'd say you had enough fun for one day."

He and Buzzy slammed the storm cellar doors. A rusty lock and chain were wrapped around the handles. Fargo secured the doors with the chain and slapped the lock between the links, snapping the lock shut and effectively sealing Dexter inside.

Buzzy said, "You sure it's wise to lock him down there? What iffen we all git killed?"

"I think we're all hopin' that doesn't happen," Fargo said.

15

Dexter pushed up uselessly on the storm cellar doors. All he got for his troubles was a faceful of dirt and a few dull streaks of sunlight poking between the boards.

He screamed out for help a few times, but knew it was useless. Fargo, as usual, was being true to his stubborn character. Dexter cursed the day he'd gone to work at Livermore and Beedle, cursed Mr. Huffington for sending him here, cursed the landlord who demanded money every month, cursed his dead father and Otis Fleagle and everyone else he could think of.

He looked around the storm cellar. A few broken pieces of furniture lay scattered on the dirt floor, an ancient oil lantern hung from a bent nail in the ceiling. At least it was cooler down here. Dexter spotted a filthy old blanket lying in one corner. He went over and grabbed it. Underneath a slithering family of snakes hissed indignantly at him. Dexter dropped the blanket and retreated to the far end of the cellar. He sat, trying to ignore the pain in his rump, and tried to make himself comfortable. Within two minutes he was asleep.

He was dreaming of burying his face in Prudie Fisher's delectable breasts when the sound of gunshots woke him. He wasn't too sure how long he'd been asleep; it could have been an hour, it could have been five minutes. He scurried up the steps and tried to peek through the wooden slats of the cellar door, but could see little. He did, however, hear the exploding rifle shots and snippets of talk, like, "Go around back, Chigger!" and "The old buzzard's firing from the water tower!"

Damn that Fargo, depriving Dexter of the opportunity to see firsthand the Siege of Paradise, as he would refer to it when he wrote it up. He longed to be a part of the action. And, as was lately becoming customary, the action very shortly came to him.

He heard two shots from directly above him—the roar was damn near deafening—and the sounds of chains being pulled away. Finally, Dexter thought, Fargo had had a change of heart.

But it wasn't Fargo who flung open the cellar doors and leaped down onto the hard ground; it was none other than Earl Danby, doubtless looking for a place to hide until the shooting stopped, the gutless puke. Dexter scanned the dark space desperately for something to use as a weapon before Earl's eyes could adjust to the darkness. He spotted a chair leg and went for it, diving across the cellar. His intentions were good; his timing was lousy. Earl spotted him and jumped on Dexter's back before he could grab the chair leg.

"Well, looky what we got us here," Earl said.

Earl was maybe an inch or two shorter than Dexter and maybe ten pounds lighter, but he more than made up for it in meanness. He got his forearm around Dexter's gullet and squeezed, trying to snap his neck. With one hand free, Earl went for his pistol and was about to use it to cave in Dexter's skull. Dexter reached up and grabbed a greasy clump of Earl's hair and yanked with every last ounce of strength he could muster. Earl cried out in pain and whacked Dexter's hand with the butt of the pistol. Dexter held firm, though, and somehow, some way, using muscles he never knew he had, managed to topple Earl onto his side. Earl's pistol went flying off into the darkness of the cellar.

Dexter pounced, landing on top of Earl, and they rolled around in the dank, dark cellar locked in a death grip and somehow, at least for the moment, Dexter ended up on top.

He wrapped his hands around Earl's scrawny throat. Earl, in turn, jammed his thumbs into Dexter's eyes. Though it took some effort, he managed to pry Earl's thumbs loose before his eyeballs popped out of his head like a pair of hard-boiled eggs. His victory was short-lived; Earl lashed out with a right hook that took Dexter flat on the chin. It was like Harvey's crap game fight all over again.

Dexter's grip loosened on Earl's throat. Earl pushed Dexter off and scampered away, looking anxiously for his gun. He spotted it a few feet away, next to the filthy old blanket in the corner. Dexter knew in that split second that if Earl got his grubby paws on the gun, he was better than dead.

Inching forward with Dexter on his back, Earl reached out and brushed the butt of the pistol with the tips of his fingers. Gritting his teeth and groaning with the effort, Earl's fingers closed around the pistol. He pulled it toward him and, when he had it firmly in hand, poked the barrel an inch from Dexter's head.

Dexter knew all too well that he had only one chance at surviving. With one hand he grabbed Earl's greasy hair again and yanked his head back. With his other, he grabbed the filthy blanket and tossed it aside. Underneath, the family of rattlesnakes hissed. Dexter slammed Earl face first down into the nest of rattlers, then threw himself off Earl's back and retreated safely away.

The rattlesnakes—there were half a dozen of them at least—coiled and buried their fangs into Earl's nose and eyes and cheeks. Earl's high-pitched screams could doubtless be heard in the next county. He managed to roll onto his back, the snakes still affixed to his face, and vainly tried to pull them off, which only pissed them off even more. They attacked his hands and his neck, biting him repeatedly. For one crazy moment, Dexter remembered a picture he'd seen in a book on Greek mythology about Medusa, the ugly lady who had snakes for hair and turned anyone who looked at her into stone. Earl looked a lot like that picture, the snakes hanging from his face and scalp as they injected their deadly venom into his veins.

Earl fell backward and started twitching uncontrollably, his head shaking like an old man with the palsy. The snakes slithered away into the safety of the dark corner. A minute later, Earl was dead. Dexter stood and nudged Earl's body with the tip of his shoe. He was satisfied that Earl Danby wouldn't be going anywhere except straight to Hell where he belonged. Earl was even uglier in death; his eyes were still open, his mouth twisted in agony.

Dexter picked up Earl's pistol and made his way up the stairs into daylight.

Ten minutes earlier, the Danbys had galloped into Paradise and weren't quite prepared for what awaited them. Specifically, what awaited them was a whole lot of nothing.

The town was seemingly deserted except for one mangy old mutt who was licking his sweetmeats in the middle of Main Street. Other than the old cur, though, it was quiet enough to hear a sparrow break wind.

Earl Danby hated dogs. He shot the old mutt and laughed when the creature yelped in pain, rolled over, and died. The echo of the gunshot faded, and it was quiet again.

"They all musta cleared out when they heared we was coming," Chigger said.

There were only six of them now; they'd left Lyle Gorch and Packy Gribble for the buzzards. They were all in moods more foul than usual. Rounding up their horses took longer than it should have, and they'd gotten no sleep the night before. Violet was in a particularly nasty humor; there was a huge, ugly purple lump on her jaw where Fargo had kicked her, loosening a couple of back teeth. She'd spit blood for hours and her mouth hurt something fierce. She also had a black eye, where Hoke had belted her for letting Fargo get to the horses.

"I don't like the looks of this, Hoke," Nathan Gribble said. "Something ain't right."

"Shut up," Hoke said, but the truth was, he didn't like the looks of this, either. Sure, they'd ridden into small towns like this one where the folks had gotten wind of their arrival and fled in terror. Something was different this time, though he couldn't quite put his finger on it.

Hoke spurred his horse and trotted a little further down Main Street. As was their custom, the others followed, putting some distance between themselves.

Crouching low on the church steeple, Buzzy Oathammer waited for the signal. He prayed Fargo's plan would work. Lying flat on top of the bakery, across the street from Sneed Hearn's saloon and five buildings down from the church, Fargo watched the Danbys make their way warily down the street. He wanted them all together, not spread out as they were now. Nashville Katz, Fargo saw, was inside the town hall. He'd broken a pane of glass on the window that faced the street. He, too, waited for the signal.

Fargo was banking on one thing—outlaws were always thirsty.

He watched as Hoke and the others dismounted. Fargo could have given the signal to start shooting now, but he decided to wait.

Hoke walked through the batwing saloon doors. The others followed, except for Violet, who stayed behind as the lookout. So far, so good, Fargo thought.

Inside, the Danbys were greeted by a somewhat unusual sight: Edwin Fix, Sneed Hearn's dirty apron tied around his waist, was wiping the bar with a damp cloth. The place was utterly deserted.

Fix looked up at Hoke and the others. He grinned and said, "Mornin', gentlemen. What can I get y'all?"

Hoke said, "Kinda quiet around here."

"Yup," Fix said. "Church picnic today, over to Wagon-wood Ridge. Everyone and his mother went. 'Ceptin' me, of course. I don't ever close my saloon iffen I can help it."

"You got any idear who we is?" Earl Danby asked.

"Nope," Fix said. "And as long as you're money's green, friend, I figure it ain't none of my concern. I'll say this though—you boys look mighty parched. Sure I can't draw y'all a nice cool beer?"

"I'll have one," Jeeter Gorch said, and Nathan Gribble seconded the motion.

"No," Hoke ordered. "Nothin' for any of 'em."

"Aw, c'mon, Hoke," Chigger protested. "One beer is all—cain't hurt nothin'."

They bellied up to the bar, all except Hoke. His dark, suspicious eyes darted around the saloon. "Somethin' ain't right here," he said under his breath.

The others ignored him as Fix reached under the bar and started filling mugs with beer. They had no way of knowing, of course, that Edwin Fix, at Fargo's suggestion, had spiked the barrel of beer with three bottles of laudanum, commandeered from Doc Phipps's office.

Marshal Fix drew five beers, handing them off to Earl, Chigger, Nathan Gribble, and Jeeter Gorch. The beers were downed in one gulp. Only Hoke did not drink.

"Another?" Fix asked, and didn't wait for an answer. He drew four more beers and the outlaws drank, a little slower this time. The aroma of laudanum filled the saloon. Hoke's well trained nose worked furiously; he grabbed the beer mug from Chigger and sniffed the contents.

"Spit out that beer, you prairie rats!" he ordered. "This beer's been doped."

They all dropped their beer mugs, but the damage had been done. The effects of the laudanum, was creeping up on all of them except for Hoke. Hoke grabbed Fix's skinny necktie and yanked him forward so that they were nose to nose.

"What'd you put in that beer, sidewinder?" he asked.

"Nothin'," Fix said, and reached under the bar for his pistol. Hoke pushed him away, drew his gun, and fired two shots into the marshal. One hit him in the upper shoulder, the other took him in the chest. Fix crumpled to the floor behind the bar.

"On your horses, now," Hoke ordered, and the Danby gang made a beeline for the swinging saloon doors. They stumbled out onto the street, dodging and weaving, the effects of the laudanum well upon them.

"Now!" Fargo shouted.

The bullets came flying in from everywhere. Jeeter Gorch took a hunk of lead an inch above his left eye, courtesy of Katz's Remington shotgun. He'd been aiming for Hoke, but Jeeter had gotten in the way.

They scattered, not bothering with their horses. Buzzy, from the steeple, got Chigger in his gunsights and brought him down with two in the spine. He went next for Earl, but the little bastard had disappeared behind the church.

Violet Danby hid behind a water tank and got Buzzy in her sights as he reloaded. She squeezed off two shots. The first shot sailed harmlessly over his head. The second one took him in the throat, the force slamming him backward. He hit the sloped side of the steeple and slid to the floor.

Violet turned her attention to the figure firing at her from inside the town hall. They'd been set up beautifully, she'd give them that. She had no idea where Hoke and Earl had gotten to, and at that moment it didn't much matter. She thought she recognized the guy firing at her—it was that crazy man from last night. She fired at him again; the shot went wild through the window, two feet above his head. The bullet hit the thin chain that supported a small chandelier suspended from the crossbeams. The chain snapped, sending the chandelier crashing down on Nashville Katz's head, knocking him cold.

Katz never saw it coming.

It was just Fargo, Hoke, and Violet now. Earl was nowhere to be seen.

The rest happened quickly. Fargo was huddled in the doorway of the bakery. Violet was behind the horse trough. Hoke's whereabouts were a mystery.

Across the street, the window of Toody's Café shattered. Fargo and Violet both fired in that direction, unaware that Hoke had tossed a rock through it to get their attention. His plan worked. Fargo, standing in the doorway, fired two shots at Violet, who'd jumped up from behind the horse trough to fire at the imaginary enemy by the café. Both of Fargo's shots slammed into Violet's pretty little head, killing her on the spot. She fell into the trough, turning the water deep-red.

A shot rang out across the street from the café, and Fargo felt himself being slammed against the wall. The Colt flew out of his hand as he fell flat on his back. Hoke Danby's bullet had taken him squarely in the right shoulder, an inch below the armpit.

He flailed helplessly for the Colt. He'd left his Henry inside the bakery, a stupid move now that he realized it.

Hoke Danby walked briskly across the street, never taking his eyes off Fargo. He kicked Fargo's Colt out of the way, then stepped hard on Fargo's shoulder just for the hell of it. Fargo winced in pain until Hoke backed off and started reloading his gun.

"You kilt Violet," Hoke said. "A real waste. That gal could work you so hard your eyeballs got sucked into the back of your head." If he was upset about Violet's death, or that of any of his relations, for that matter, he wasn't showing it.

"You set her up to get killed," Fargo said. "Your own sister. You knew what you were doing all along." He was sweating and his face was pale from the loss of blood.

"Yeah, well, a man's gotta do what he's gotta do," Hoke

said, spinning the chamber of his pistol. "You an' your pals did a pretty good number on us. But not good enough."

He pointed the gun an inch from Fargo's face and pulled back the hammer. Before he could squeeze the trigger, a shot rang out behind him, spinning him around from the force so that he was facing the man who'd shot him. The pistol dropped from his hand.

Ten yards away, Dexter, holding Earl Danby's pistol, fired another shot at Hoke Danby, hitting him an inch below the left eye. Still Hoke didn't drop. Dexter shot him again, near the belly. Hoke weaved back and forth, a look of astonishment on his face.

He said to Dexter, "You killed me, you rat bastard. You really did kill me."

"You're not a nice person," Dexter said. "Not nice at all."

"Yeah," Hoke said. "I hear that a lot."

Hoke crumpled into a heap on the dusty street, his lifeless carcass already drawing horseflies. Dexter went over to Fargo and helped the tall man to his feet.

Dexter asked, "I *was* supposed to shoot him, wasn't I?"

"Yeah, you were," Fargo said.

Nashville Katz sauntered out of the town hall, rubbing his head. He saw Hoke lying dead in the middle of the street and said to Fargo, "You're a grave disappointment to me, Mr. Fargo. You knew I wanted to dispose of Hoke Danby myself."

"Don't blame me," Fargo said. "Our friend Dexter here did the deed."

Dexter grinned weakly and said, "I'm sorry, Mr. Katz. He was going to kill Mr. Fargo."

"I guess I forgive you then," Katz said.

They made their way over to the saloon. Behind the bar, slumped on the floor, Marshal Fix lay still. He opened one eye and said, "I'm getting too old for this."

"Aren't we all," Fargo replied.

16

Dexter and Fargo waited at the train station. The Fort Worth–bound train was due in a couple of minutes.

Buzzy Oathammer was hobbling around on a wooden crutch, trying not to fall over. Nashville Katz was talking to the stationmaster, inquiring about a train to somewhere or other.

It was three days later. There'd been a big celebration for the four men who'd beaten the Danby gang, with cotton candy and barbecue and free-flowing whiskey, just as promised. The people of Paradise were grateful to Fargo and the others for saving their town from disaster. Marshal Fix was recuperating over at Ma Fisher's boardinghouse. Dexter had not seen Prudie since that fateful morning when she'd initiated him to the joys of female flesh.

Mr. Muckle had cheerfully supplied Dexter with a brand new suit, a pair of shoes a size too large, and a big cowboy hat four sizes too large, saying, "You're a true hero of the West now, son."

Dexter put the hat on. It sank over his head and bent his ears in half.

"It's what we call a ten-gallon hat," Mr. Muckle explained.

"I think five gallons would have been plenty," Dexter said.

Things in Paradise were more or less back to normal. It was time for Dexter to go home.

"Guess it'll be good to finally see Brooklyn again," Fargo said.

"I guess," Dexter said, scanning the street for any sign of Prudie. Just around the time the train appeared on the western horizon, Dexter spotted her. She was walking arm in arm with a good looking man twice Dexter's size and about five years older. Dexter's heart sank.

They strolled over to the bench where Dexter and Fargo now sat. Prudie said, "Going home, Mr. Tritt?"

"Might as well," he said. "There's nothing keeping me here, is there?"

"I guess not," Prudie said. "Have a pleasant journey."

She walked off with her new beau. Dexter watched them go and sighed deeply, saying, "I don't imagine I'll ever understand women."

"It's best not to try," Fargo said.

"Don't take it to hard, boy," Buzzy said. "Truth is, Miss Prudie enjoys breakin' hearts. She'd have brought you nothin' but misery."

"That kind of misery I could live with," Dexter said.

Presently, the train pulled in. Nashville Katz came strolling over, holding a ticket.

Fargo asked him, "You clearing out, too?"

"My work here is done," he said. "And I could definitely use a nice vacation. I thought I might accompany Mr. Tritt here back to New York."

As things turned out, there was a sizable reward due to them for killing the Danbys; the various bounties amounted to more than $10,000. "You're both due a cut of the reward money," Fargo told them. "Let me know where to send it."

"I'll let you know, you shouldn't worry," Katz said.

He shook hands with Fargo and Buzzy, saying, "Goodbye, gentlemen. It's been a true pleasure working with you."

"Good-bye, Nashville," Buzzy said. "We shore did kick us some Danby butt, didn't we?"

"It was a goodness," Katz agreed, and climbed aboard the train. "Coming, Mr. Tritt?"

Dexter grabbed his new suitcase, which was filled with a week's worth of new clothes, all courtesy, again, of Muckle's Mercantile.

"Good-bye, Buzzy," Dexter said. "I hope you feel better very soon."

"You take care, young feller," Buzzy said, pumping Dexter's hand. "Give 'em what fer back East."

"I'll do my best," Dexter said, and turned to Fargo. "Good-bye, Mr. Fargo. Take care of yourself."

"You too, Dexter," Fargo said with a smile. "You done real good. You came to Texas a boy. You're going home a man. I reckon I owe you one."

"That's okay," Dexter said. "You'd have done the same for me."

Dexter started to board the train. Fargo said to him, "You still got that book contract on you?"

Dexter turned and said, "As a matter of fact, I do."

"Like I said, I owe you one," Fargo said. "Give it here."

Dexter pulled the slightly tattered paper from his coat pocket and handed it to Fargo, who scanned it quickly and said, "Got a pen?"

Dexter did. He gave it to Fargo, who said, "I reckon I'll write up some junk for you, and you turn it into English. I'll sign this on just one condition."

"What's that?" Dexter asked.

"If you ever stop workin' for Livermore and Beedle, the deal's off," Fargo said. "Write that into this here agreement, okay?"

"Yes, sir," Dexter said happily.

Fargo and Buzzy watched the train disappear into the flat Texas plain, belching black smoke into the afternoon.

"Don't know about you," Fargo said to him, "but I might just miss that boy some."

"Yeah, me too," Buzzy said.

"Care for a drink?" Fargo asked. "I'm buyin'."

"Ain't never turned down a drink in my life," Buzzy said, and together they headed off to Sneed Hearn's saloon.

LOOKING FORWARD!

**The following is the opening
section from the next novel in the exciting
Trailsman series from Signet:**

**THE TRAILSMAN #242
WYOMING WHIRLWIND**

*Wyoming, 1859—
Death makes good on but one promise:
Both the rich and poor
shall see it kept.*

Thunder Basin in eastern Wyoming had never looked more deserted. The vast grasslands stretched to the horizon like a green, endlessly heaving ocean. Skye Fargo drew rein and dismounted to give his stallion a rest. He swiped at the sweat beading his forehead as he studied the expanse in front of him for sign of a buffalo herd. Killing one of the big wooly beasts provided more meat than he needed, but it was an easier kill than going after the wily rabbits that poked out their long-eared heads from hidden burrows, then lit out faster than a bullet could follow.

Fargo figured to kill a buffalo, eat his fill, and dress out the rest. He wasn't all that far from Newcastle and could sell the meat there for another month of supplies.

"I want water, too." he said to his Ovaro, patting the horse on the neck. The stallion tossed its head and tried to rear. This unusual behavior put Fargo on guard. When he saw the horse's nostrils flare and the whites around its eyes show, he knew something was seriously amiss.

Hand resting on the Colt holstered at his side, Fargo turned his sharp eyes out across the gently waving grasslands. Thunder Basin was not living up to its name. For three days Fargo had ridden without spotting so much as a cloud above the increasingly sere grass. He had seen drier stretches but not recently. There had to be something more than a storm cloud randomly tossing off lightning he could not see or hear that spooked the normally steady horse.

Fargo smelled the prairie fire before he saw it.

A cold chill ran down his spine. Indians and outlaws held no terror for him. He had faced grizzly bears and had walked away. Blizzards and wind storms did not frighten him unduly. They were natural occurrences, however violent, and a smart man survived them. But not a prairie fire. They took on a life of their own, devouring everything in their path. Worst of all for anyone trapped on the prairie, the path of the fire could change on a dime. One instant the fire might be burning east. A gust of wind might set it burning north faster than any man could escape—or the fire could double back over terrain it had already charred, as if leery of leaving a single blade of grass untouched.

Skye Fargo was known as the Trailsman because of his skills, but even the Trailsman wisely gave way before a prairie fire. The only safe place when the fires raced with the wind across a broad grassland was far, far away.

Fargo mounted and turned his paint's face away from the greasy gray smoke he spotted on the horizon to the north. The smell of burning vegetation filled his nostrils now and mingled with it came another unmistakable odor—burned meat. The buffalos he had sought must have been caught in the fire as well.

Casting a quick look over his shoulder to locate the herd brought Fargo up short. In the distance he spotted a lone rider.

"Damnation," he muttered. Fargo tugged on the Ovaro's reins and got the horse headed back in the direction they had been traveling before he had scented the fire. The horse balked, but Fargo kept it moving down the gently sloping hill and out across Thunder Basin.

Fargo put his heels to the horse's flanks, urging as much speed as he could from the powerful animal. He kept his head down but looked up now and again to be sure he headed in the proper direction. Huge walls of billowing black smoke rose on his right, getting closer but still not an immediate threat.

"Turn back!" Fargo shouted. "Fire! Look behind you!"

The rider straightened and looked around as if shaken out of deep thought. Then he reined in.

"Hello," the man called. "What did you say?"

"Fire!" shouted Fargo. He pointed frantically. The advancing wall of roiling smoke now showed faint specks of bright orange and yellow flames in its midst. The fire was still miles off, but Fargo knew how fast a prairie fire moved.

Faster than a horse could ever hope to run.

"What? What's that?" The man seemed too bullheaded to acknowledge what was obvious to Fargo.

Fargo pointed toward the unmistakable wall of smoke now laced with bright tongues of flame. The wind was picking up and blew directly at the man's back. Fargo might have been safe if he had not seen the rider and come to warn him. But he would never have slept well again if he had abandoned the man to his fate.

"We have to get out of the path of the fire. It'll kill everything in its path."

"Fire? I thought that was a thunderstorm. It's been so dry, I reckoned on getting a little wet."

"You're going to get a lot burned unless you hightail it now," Fargo said, coming up beside the man. He gave the rider a quick once-over and wondered what he had found out here in the basin. The man's clothing was impeccably clean and looked brand-new—store-bought new. He wore his fancy beaver felt hat pulled down at a jaunty angle on his forehead. There was hardly enough dust on the broad brim for the hat to have been out of the box longer than a day or two. Shiny boots with flashy patterns gleamed in the gathering smoke, and riding at the man's hip was a Smith & Wesson that had never been fired.

"I suppose we should get out of the way of the fire, then," the man said. He twisted around and thrust out his hand. "My name's Paul Hancock."

"Mine's Fargo. Now ride like you mean it." Fargo hesitated a moment, then asked, "You *can* ride?"

"Why, of course I can," Hancock said, irritated. "I can ride as good as you, I am sure. Although that is a mighty fine specimen of horseflesh you're astride."

Fargo looked at him as if he lost his senses. He stood in the stirrups and got a good look at the countryside. Continuing in the direction Hancock had been riding would mean their deaths within the hour. Fargo knew he could never retrace his path to the rise. That was all uphill and his Ovaro, strong as it was, had tired racing across the grassland to reach Paul Hancock.

"That way," Fargo said, coming to a quick decision. The

terrain sloped downward slightly, possibly draining into a stream. If so, that gave them even better protection against the fire devouring the grasslands to the east. The fire might jump a small stream, but if the land drained into a river, they were safe after they crossed it.

"What's in that direction?" Hancock asked, still not acknowledging the danger they faced. Fargo already imagined the heat turning his six-shooter too hot to touch, his shirt smoldering, his flesh turning red and then blistering.

"If we're lucky, a river," Fargo said. "If we're not lucky in finding water, we still might escape."

"Why such a hurry?" Hancock asked as Fargo galloped off.

Fargo looked over his shoulder as he rode and wondered if he would have to rope and hogtie Hancock to get him out of danger. The man was totally oblivious to everything happening around him. Fargo had seen toddlers with better sense than the fancy-dressed man.

He heaved a sigh of relief when he saw Hancock snap the reins and get his mare into a trot. When it became apparent Fargo was leaving him farther behind by the minute, Hancock pulled the new hat down around his ears and spurred his horse into a gallop.

Fargo knew the danger of running across a grassy stretch like this. Prairie-dog holes, rabbit burrows, snake holes . . . all afforded excellent ways for a horse barreling along to break a leg. It was a risk he had to take now if he wanted to keep his hide from being roasted like a pheasant on a cooking spit.

"This is great fun!" called Hancock, pulling even with Fargo. The man's horse was fresher, not having galloped miles out onto the prairie to warn a damned fool of the danger. Fargo was glad he had not simply fired a warning shot but had come to fetch the man. Hancock would have ignored gunfire, thinking it was nothing but thunder from a nonexistent storm. How anyone could be so ignorant and still be alive was beyond Fargo.

He hunkered down and knew the Ovaro would carry him to safety. The fire was no longer overtaking them. By riding at an angle to the fire line, he took a chance, but the downhill slope made the effort easier for the paint.

A loud cry of surprise followed by a sound that turned Fargo sick inside forced him to slow the Ovaro's retreat, then circle and backtrack.

Paul Hancock lay flat on his back staring up at the smoky sky. His chest heaved as he struggled to catch his breath. He had been thrown from his horse and had had the wind knocked from his lungs. Otherwise, he appeared all right.

The horse wasn't as lucky. Fargo had heard the sound of a horse's leg breaking too often not to recognize it instantly. The whinnying and frightened snorts completed the sad story. He had worried about his horse stepping into a hole. Hancock's had. Whether the other man had been too inexperienced to avoid the prairie-dog town or had not seen it in his rush to keep up with Fargo hardly mattered.

"Wh-what happened?" Hancock asked, struggling to sit up.

"Your horse broke its leg," Fargo said. "You want to handle it?" He studied the man for a moment and couldn't tell if the fall had shaken him up so much he didn't understand, or if he simply was faced with a situation beyond his experience. There wasn't time to discuss it.

Fargo drew his Colt, aimed, and fired. The bullet took down the pain-racked horse instantly, putting it out of its misery.

"You shot my horse!" shouted Hancock, fumbling for his Smith & Wesson.

"You looked too shook up to do it yourself," Fargo said. "Climb up behind me."

"My gear," Hancock said, stumbling forward.

"It'll get burned up with both of us if you don't mount fast." Fargo held out his hand for Hancock. The man returned his six-shooter to its holster and let Fargo help him up. The Ovaro staggered slightly under the doubled weight, then took off with its usual even gait.

"How can you be so sure the fire will come this way?" Hancock asked.

"You can see it, feel it, smell it, and taste it," Fargo said. He brought the Ovaro to a trot and kept it at this gait because any faster would exhaust it. The last thing Fargo wanted was to be afoot on the prairie with a fire burning the flesh at the back of his neck.

"Oh," was all Hancock said. The man fell silent as they made their way at an angle to the fire. By the time they reached the dubious safety of the small stream, the crackle and snap of flames were easily heard.

"Rest for a few minutes," Fargo ordered the man. "Get yourself wet all over. I don't think the fire will jump the stream, but there's no reason not to give ourselves whatever advantage we can." He let his pinto drink while he walked into the knee-deep stream and then sat, taking care to hold his Colt above water as he dunked himself.

Hancock was slower to follow suit and, when he did join Fargo, forgot to draw his Smith & Wesson. He didn't notice that he had given his black-powder gun such a dousing that it probably would not fire until it had been dried carefully and reloaded. The more Fargo considered Paul Hancock, the more of a mystery the man became.

But it was a mystery to be solved later. Fifty-foot-high clouds of black smoke gusted toward the stream and through it Fargo saw real danger. The flames greedily devoured anything that grew, feeding the voracious fire.

"Let's ride," Fargo said, mounting his Ovaro and helping Hancock up behind him again. He was glad he had insisted that they soak their clothing. The heat from the approaching flames began to prickle his skin. The water would evaporate fast but might protect them long enough so they could put a few more miles between their backs and the deadly flames.

"I . . . they're so big. I've never seen a fire so big."

"It's turning, following the bank of the stream," Fargo said. They were safe—or as safe as they could be until the prairie fire burned itself out entirely.

"Where are you heading?" Hancock asked.

"Away from the fire. Far away," Fargo said. "Do you have somewhere better to go?"

"I'm not sure, but I think camp is in this direction."

The notion Hancock was out on the prairie with others like him made Fargo laugh. He knew it was as much release from the strain of getting away from the fire as anything, and he did not want to make fun of Hancock, but the thought of a dozen more dandies like Hancock struck him as funny.

"It's not?" asked Hancock. "I got turned around while I was hunting for buffalo."

"You're asking me where your camp is?" Fargo continued to be amazed at the man's ignorance. Usually, anyone this witless died fast on the frontier.

"Can you find it? There are ten or so of us. Two wagons, quite a few horses. I remember looking up this morning and seeing twin peaks like those in the distance."

"To the north?"

"I suppose," Hancock said, obviously not sure of directions. "Yes, that way. Those are definitely the hills I saw."

"What brings you out to Wyoming?" Fargo asked. He held the Ovaro to a slow walk now to conserve the horse's strength. The fire was burning along the stream, giving them a significant margin of safety now, but he wasn't one to take needless risks.

"Hunting," Hancock said. "For buffalo."

"You're a buffalo hunter? You don't look much like one." Fargo laughed and added, "You don't smell much like one, either. Usually, I have to ride upwind to even get near them after only a day or two of serious shooting."

"Because I bathe is no reason to mock me," Hancock said stiffly.

"I wasn't twitting you. I was only observing that you didn't smell bad." Fargo kept it to himself that Hancock smelled like a whore all dabbed up with cheap French perfume.

"I apologize for being so testy," Hancock said quickly. "This entire ordeal has agitated me."

"Fire will do that," Fargo agreed.

"My horse," Hancock said. "You shot my horse."

"Look," Fargo said, growing exasperated with the man's attitude. "You were all shook up because your horse threw you. I would have let you shoot your own horse if you'd been up to it, but the fire was getting mighty hot."

"Shoot it! Why kill a perfectly good horse?"

"It broke its leg. It was the only merciful thing to do, unless you know some way of putting a splint on a horse's foreleg. I don't."

"That was an expensive horse," Hancock grumbled.

Fargo was at a loss to understand what was going on.

Before he could figure out how to ask without raising the prickly man's ire, Hancock bounced up and down and pointed.

"There! There's the camp."

Fargo could hardly believe his eyes as they followed the game trail around a hill into a hollow. Two wagons were parked off to one side, but what wagons! They gleamed in the sun like the finest mahogany bar he had ever seen. Getting closer, Fargo saw the wagons *were* made of mahogany. But the men in the camp were even more of a puzzle.

They were dressed in fancy duds, one decked out like a butler in a gray cutaway coat. His white shirt had been boiled and starched so it was as stiff as the man's spine. Stepping forward as if walking barefoot on broken glass, the man looked at Fargo as if he had bitten into a sour persimmon.

"Good morning, sir." His sharp black eyes fixed on Fargo.

"Reckon you're where you belong," Fargo said, looking over the camp and its pristine equipment. Everything he saw was new and expensive.

"Thanks," Hancock said, jumping down clumsily. "Why don't you stay for a bite to eat? It's the least we can do for you."

"Sir," the liveried man said, looking even more disgusted. "I am not sure Mr. Compton would approve. After all, this . . . person . . . is wearing the skin of a dead animal."

Fargo looked at his buckskins. They had been new at the beginning of spring, and he had only worn them for a few months. He knew better than to argue the point. These were strange folks with strange ways, and he wanted nothing to do with them.

"That's all right, Hancock," Fargo said. "Steer clear of that fire and you'll be fine."

"Thanks, Fargo. I appreciate what you've done for me." With that Hancock turned and ignored Fargo.

Fargo turned his Ovaro's face and started for the mountains to the north, away from the flames. When the fire burned itself out it would leave no forage for his horse. Worse than that, it would have driven any buffalo ahead of it, forcing him to run them down. Better to find another herd that hadn't been frightened off by fire.

Fargo had ridden only ten minutes when he heard a horse's hooves pounding hard behind him. He turned and saw a frantic Paul Hancock riding for him, shouting incoherently.

Not sure what the problem was, Fargo reined in and waited for the man to catch up.

"Fargo, Fargo, you've got to help! My sister! She's back there!"

"Back where? In camp?"

"No, no, Melissa is out on the range. In the fire! She's in front of the fire! Help me find her before it's too late!"